"We need to set some ground rules."

David Prescott's hard blue eyes dissected Diana. "First, the furniture in the carriage house—I expect it to be left in the same condition you find it."

"What do you think I'm going to do? Gnaw on it?"

The look he gave her was corroding. "Lock the gate behind you whenever you go out or come in. That's not just a suggestion. That's an order." He tossed her a large key.

Diana considered flinging the key back at him. This man was insufferable!

His eyes swept over her, missing nothing. "And one final point . . ."

"Yes, what is it *now?*"

"I don't care much for insolence, either."

Shannon Waverly lives in Massachusetts with her husband, a high school English teacher. Their two children are both in college. Shannon wrote her first romance at the age of twelve, and she's been writing ever since. She says that in her first year of college, she joined the literary magazine and ''promptly submitted the most pompous allegory imaginable. The editor at the time just as promptly rejected it. But he also asked me out; he and I have now been married twenty-one years.''

Books by Shannon Waverly

HARLEQUIN ROMANCE
3072—A SUMMER KIND OF LOVE

Don't miss any of our special offers. Write to us at the following address for information on our newest releases.

Harlequin Reader Service
P.O. Box 1397, Buffalo, NY 14240
Canadian address: P.O. Box 603,
Fort Erie, Ont. L2A 5X3

NO TRESPASSING
Shannon Waverly

TORONTO • NEW YORK • LONDON
AMSTERDAM • PARIS • SYDNEY • HAMBURG
STOCKHOLM • ATHENS • TOKYO • MILAN

ISBN 0-373-03150-5

Harlequin Romance first edition September 1991

NO TRESPASSING

CHAPTER ONE

THE CLOSER DIANA GOT to Newport the more apprehensive she became. Vague intuitive fears feathered through her stomach and tied her muscles into knots.

She knew she was being ridiculous, and she told herself so repeatedly. She was merely on her way to Rhode Island to spend the next eight weeks tutoring one sweet nonthreatening fifteen-year-old who'd failed sophomore English—and that was all.

But no matter how often she tried to reassure herself, she knew that was *not* all. From the moment she'd accepted the position, she had been hearing things, catching strange innuendos....

"YOU'RE GOING TO BE tutoring the Osborne girl this summer?" Grace Mathias exclaimed not an hour after Diana had left the headmistress's office. Grace was an art instructor at Fairview Academy, the private boarding school in Vermont where Diana had been teaching for three years.

Diana dropped a heavy stack of final exam papers on the lunch table and smiled. "Pretty great, isn't it!" Cissy Osborne had been one of her favorite students the previous year, and the prospect of spending a summer with her—and getting paid for it—cheered her immensely. In addition, she'd be staying in historic Newport, Rhode Island, a place she'd always wanted to visit. Of course, there were other reasons for her wanting to get away from Vermont this summer. But she wouldn't let herself even think about those for fear they'd register on her face.

"Well, my, my!" Grace said. "My, my, my!" Then she strolled out of the faculty room, leaving Diana staring after her in bewilderment.

She poured a cup of coffee and glanced over at Mildred Price, a fellow English teacher. Mildred was at the table having lunch. "Do you have any clue what that was all about?"

"Must have something to do with the fact you'll be living with Cissy's family."

"Oh." Diana's puzzlement deepened. "But I won't really be living *with* them. They have a few rooms over their garage they're letting me use."

As Mildred chewed on her sandwich, frowning thoughtfully, Diana felt a growing uneasiness.

"Did Carrington tell you anything about them?" Mildred asked.

"A little. Cissy's an only child, and her mother's divorced. They live in Manhattan, but in the summer they go to their house in Newport. Actually, it's not Mrs. Osborne's house. It's her uncle's." Diana opened the refrigerator, found her brown bag and sat opposite Mildred.

"Did she mention that this uncle's house..."

"Cliff Haven?"

"What?"

"Cliff Haven. The house has a name." Diana smiled. She liked that idea, of naming houses. She and Skip would have to come up with a name for the farm, something more poetic than White's Dairy.

"Yes, well... did she bother to tell you that Cliff Haven is one of the Newport mansions?"

Diana had just taken a bite of her ham-and-cheese, but suddenly her jaw turned to stone.

"Surprise, surprise," Mildred said, unsmiling.

Diana took a sip of coffee and finally got the food down. "I expected something nice. I mean, most of the girls here are... Are they *that* well-to-do?"

"I expect so. They're Prescotts, you know. Osborne is Cissy's mother's married name."

"Prescotts?"

"Mm. The *steel* Prescotts."

Diana suspected she still looked baffled.

"Honestly, Diana, sometimes I wonder where you've been all your life!"

Lost within the pages of literature, she thought to say but didn't.

Neither of them was aware that Dr. Wilson, sitting in a wing chair by the window, had been listening to their conversation.

"Prescott," the old history teacher murmured, puffing on his pipe. "Now there's a name I haven't heard in a while."

Diana turned, bristling with attention. "You know these Prescotts, Doc?"

The old man chuckled. "Lord, no! Their name used to be in the papers a lot, that's all. Not that I found much in it myself, but stories about people like that sell papers, I suppose."

"People like what?" She was definitely uncomfortable now.

"Oh, you know. Wealthy people. Society people. No matter what little thing they do, it comes out looking bigger than life, doesn't it?"

Wealthy people? Society people? Diana rewrapped her sandwich and slipped it back into the bag.

"You don't hear much about them anymore, though," he continued. "Not since the old man died and there was all that infighting over—" Abruptly, he focused on her with new interest. "You say you're going to be staying with those people this summer?"

"Y-yes. Cissy failed English this term, though for the life of me I can't figure out why." For a moment, Diana's thoughts drifted back to her concern about the girl. "Anyway, her mother's asked if someone could tutor her at their summer home. It's more convenient than having her attend summer school and a lot more sensible than doubling up her English courses next year."

"Well, watch out for yourself, little lady. They spin in a whole other orbit from ordinary people like us. Of course, I could be wrong. They haven't made the news in a long time. But when they did, it was usually bad news. And that one in Newport, the uncle you mentioned—what's his name?"

"I . . . I don't know."

"Well, he always seemed to be front and center of every story. I'd give him a wide berth if I were you."

DIANA TOLD HERSELF that listening to rumor was silly. Still, during the two weeks between school closing and her leaving for Newport, she couldn't help recalling the conversations and wondering what she was getting into.

For the most part, she was barely aware of her students' backgrounds. All that really mattered was what went on in her classroom, not how much money their parents had or how many titles. She'd been raised by proud hardworking people to believe she was as good as anybody else—"and better than most," her father would always add.

And yet her imagination, which her brothers claimed would eventually be her undoing, kept getting the upper hand. There were days when, like Scott Fitzgerald, she believed rich people really were different, and that she, the gauche outsider, would spend the entire summer tripping and lost amidst their smooth sophistication.

She was ashamed of herself for giving in to such stereotypical nonsense. Not only was it uncharacteristic of her to be insecure, but it was unfair to these unknown people who would probably turn out just fine. People usually did.

She only wished the other teachers hadn't reacted so strangely. It was as if they knew something that she didn't—and should. Often she tried to recall her interview with Ms. Carrington, searching for something that might shed light on the matter. But all she remembered the headmistress saying about Cissy's family was that they were quiet private people who preferred to keep to themselves. Then she'd urged Diana to respect their desire for privacy and keep to herself, too.

"They won't even know I'm there." She nodded in complete accord.

"Good. I'm glad you understand."

But even now, paying the toll to cross the Newport Bridge, Diana still did not understand. Not fully. The only thing she was sure of was her growing uneasiness.

She shifted her red Toyota into gear and entered the flow of traffic crossing the high sweeping arc. Below her, boat-cluttered Narragansett Bay was a lifeless shade of pewter, reflecting a heavy gray sky. The hot humid day lay on Acquidneck Island like a bad mood. Before nightfall there would surely be a storm.

Diana was exhausted. Not only had she been on the road for five hours, but her brothers had kept her up well past midnight instilling innumerable fears about her spending a summer away from home. *They* had called it a going-away party.

As if she hadn't developed enough apprehensions all on her own, their gifts to her included telephone numbers of emergency ambulance services in Newport, just in case she fell seriously ill; a map of the city, all the police stations circled in red; extra money; the strongest sunscreen on the market; warnings about undertow; and to top it all off, a can of Mace because Newport was a big place, with lots of summer transients, and who knew what characters she might run into! And they said *she* had an imagination!

They meant well, all five of them, but there were times when she wished they were a little less protective. That was another reason she'd accepted the position so readily. The time had come to cut the cord. This summer would prove she could survive alone. It would also prepare them for the news she had to tell them when she returned, that she had already signed a lease on her own apartment.

She would miss Skip tremendously. They were the last two left in the farmhouse where their parents had raised them all, but it was time she moved on, away even from him. He would be marrying in the fall, and though he and Vicki pleaded with her to stay, she couldn't help feeling like extra baggage.

She supposed her brothers' protectiveness was natural, she being the only girl in the family and the youngest child, besides. Added to that, she knew she'd given them reason—like all the school-yard fights they'd rescued her from, all that misdirected anger the year their mother died.

And then there was the more recent matter of Ron Frasier. Even now, a year after he'd left her, she still felt a stab of embarrassed pain when she thought about Ron.

How could she have been so wrong about another human being? It wasn't as if she'd been a total innocent, falling for the first guy to pay her attention. She'd gone out with lots of guys. But she'd really thought this relationship was special. It was the mature relationship she'd always dreamed of having after college, after she was settled into a career.

She'd been teaching at Fairview for half a year when they started dating. He was something of a local luminary, with his drop-dead smile, his "power" wardrobe, and his ability to climb the management rungs of the largest bank in the area. Six months later, he'd asked her to marry him.

She glanced in the rearview mirror as she swung off the bridge. Her face looked strained and too pale.

Well, at least he hadn't left her standing at the altar. At least he'd had the decency to call a week ahead of time to let her know he was bowing out. She winced, remembering the shock she'd felt as his words sank in, that panicky bottoming-out feeling in the pit of her stomach.

He'd said he was sorry, but they really weren't cut out to be married to each other. What they wanted from life was just too different; *they* were too different, and she would thank him some day. Then he'd left town for a few weeks, leaving her to unravel a wedding that had taken almost a year to arrange. That was one time, she supposed, when she'd been lucky to have such a large meddlesome family. Somehow, they got her through the ordeal.

A short while later school reopened and plunged her into its blessedly hectic routine. And after a couple of months she realized with relief and surprise that she was over Ron. She even reached the point where, seeing him dash around town in his three-piece suits and rented Mercedes, she wondered why she'd ever fallen for him. He was right. They weren't suited to each other. The woman he started dating right after their split—or maybe even before—was far more his type. She was older, higher up the corporate ladder, and a much quicker route than Diana to the life-style he obviously thought he deserved.

Getting over Ron hadn't turned out to be half the problem she'd originally envisioned. The problem that did develop, though, was everyone's subsequent attitude toward her. Poor Diana! Left in the lurch while Ron paraded around town with his new woman! She might be over the love she'd felt for him, but this pity, encountered almost every day, would not let her get over her anger or embarrassment.

Even more upsetting than the pity was everyone's concern over her empty love life. In this matter her brothers were the chief offenders. She'd started dating, but they were sporadic experimental excursions at best. Each time, she'd returned home convinced she wasn't ready to get involved again. Then Andy had arranged a date with one of his work buddies, and George had invited her over to meet his unmarried neighbor. Soon life became a gauntlet of blind dates. She felt a pressure to be happy, happy with some man. But why did her brothers assume she couldn't be happy alone? Did they think she was turning into an old maid, an old spinster schoolteacher?

Funny thing was, lately she was beginning to believe it herself. Many of the men she'd dated were quite nice, and she'd tried to like them. But by the second or third date, she'd known their relationship had no future. She'd felt herself pulling away, shutting them out. The whole ordeal of dating seemed, well, ridiculous to her, distasteful. She wanted nothing to do with it. Maybe she was just shell-shocked and in time would get over her distrust and this numbness she felt toward the opposite sex. But in the meantime, all she wanted was to be left alone.

When Ms. Carrington offered her the job in Newport, Diana saw it as a godsend. It was the perfect escape from her worrying hovering family—and exactly the right place to ride out the anniversary of her almost-wedding. She needed time alone to heal.

Diana pulled to the side of the road and checked her map. She would be arriving a day or two before the family, but she preferred it that way. She wanted to be fully settled in and ready to start lessons as soon as Mrs. Osborne gave the nod. She'd been assured that a housekeeper who lived at Cliff Haven year-round would be there to meet her.

Having found her bearings, she eased back into the traffic. Within minutes, she'd reached the busy harbor district. Its shops and restaurants looked very festive in spite of the gloomy weather, which was growing gloomier by the minute, but Diana was a little too tired to fully enjoy her surroundings.

She turned up a hill, away from the harbor, and headed for Bellevue Avenue. She'd done a lot of reading about the famous Newport "cottages" since accepting this position, but driving along the tree-lined avenue, she realized how unprepared she was for the real thing. Built during the Gilded Age, they were veritable palaces of marble and granite, surrounded by lush parklike grounds. Many of them had been turned over to the Preservation Society and were open to the public, yet most were still privately owned by an elite summer colony. The Prescotts among them? she wondered. Is this what Cliff Haven would be like?

She glanced down at her rumpled khaki shorts and white tank top, clinging to her body with the muggy heat. How could she arrive at such a magnificent estate looking so bedraggled? A long filmy chiffon garmet beaded with pearls would be more appropriate. Hair done up in an elaborately coiled design—not this messy French braid hanging damply down her back. She choked out a nervous giggle.

Bellevue Avenue ended at a sharp turn and became Ocean Avenue, also marked on her map as Ten Mile Drive. Her heartbeat quickened; Cliff Haven was somewhere on this road. Appropriately enough, the ocean came into view, unbroken as far as the eye could see. Unlike the calm harbor on the other side of the island, the water here was unnervingly choppy, crashing and spraying over the huge boulders that littered the shoreline. The road was quite narrow and winding, at times bordered by a lonely stretch of marsh, an intriguing gate house or mysterious drive.

Diana could see several more mansions ahead of her, but they looked different from the ones she'd just left behind. Or was it only the harsh landscape here that made them appear so? They seemed more rugged, more like castles or fortresses, having to face the onslaught of the wind and sea so directly.

A heavy mist now blurred her windshield. The sky was bearing down hard. Somewhere in the distance, thunder rumbled. She clutched her steering wheel with fingers that had gone white, trying to keep her sense of reality from fleeing completely. It seemed that somewhere along this narrow coastal road she had lost the twentieth century—indeed, had lost America as she knew it—and had plunged into a time and place that were totally unreal.

Suddenly she spotted it, the high iron gate with the name Cliff Haven scrolled into its fretwork. Perspiration beaded on her forehead.

The house itself stood far out on a promontory overlooking the sea, a solitary bastion brooding in the mist. From the road it looked as if it were part of the cliff, having risen there at the dawn of time, stone from stone. Several tall chimneys grazed the sky, reaching up from a steep slate roof. Narrow gabled windows glinted among its towers and parapets. An English design was Diana's first impression. Rather Gothic, she thought next. No, it was downright eccentric, she concluded with a shudder.

She pulled off the road and got out of her car. This wasn't the kind of place she'd imagined. This was something else entirely. It was smaller than the grand palaces she'd glimpsed on Bellevue, darker, more isolated, and the grounds were hardly parklike. Weeds were even growing through the asphalt drive.

"They're quiet private people," Ms. Carrington had said, but now Diana wondered if the headmistress realized what sort of privacy she'd been alluding to.

Diana tried the gates, but they were firmly locked. Just above eye level, a sign stared down at her: Private Property—Keep Out—Trespassers Will Be Prosecuted. As if soundly reprimanded, Diana took an obedient step back.

With a feeling of growing helplessness, she glanced around. The estate was surrounded by an eight-foot-high wall marked at several spots with clearly lettered plates warning of electronic surveillance. Private people, indeed! She never ignored her intuition. More often than not, it proved right. And the bad feeling seeping into her bones right now was simply too real not to heed. Again she wished she knew something about Cissy's family. What had they done to be in the news? Why should the old man who owned this house be given "a wide berth"?

About ten feet inside the gate stood a sign that read Beware of the Dogs. A few feet beyond that was another, just in case some bold intruder missed the first. Ordinarily Diana loved dogs, but these persistent warnings did nothing for her sense of well-being. Trying to look as nonchalant as possible, she searched the underbrush at the base of the wall for a rock or stick, just in case one of the huge fanged three-headed creatures her imagination had spawned suddenly leapt out at her.

Then she remembered the present her brother George had given her last night. She hurried to her car and took the small can of Mace from the glove compartment. The thought of hurting an innocent animal bothered her, but if she was confronted by a pack of vicious watchdogs, perhaps the Mace would protect her.

She returned to the gate. Okay, she sighed, what next? The house was too far away for her to call out. Should she try to scale the wall? Go back to civilization and find a phone? She turned her head and quite by accident glimpsed an intercom installed in the gatepost. But of course! In order to get into a place like this, one had to announce oneself through an intercom!

Light-headed with relief, she pressed the button. She stared at the small square grille for a moment, then pressed the button again. After five minutes and several more tries, she lowered her head and groaned. Either the contraption was broken or no one was home to answer it. In her frustration, she grabbed the gate and gave it a hard angry shake.

She didn't hear the motorcycle advancing up the road, and became aware of it only when it roared off the macadam and skidded to a heart-shattering stop behind her. She spun around in blind panic just as its tall dark rider vaulted off. He flung his helmet down and started coming toward her.

In the space of a heartbeat, she took in the huge black Harley and the equally sinister-looking man it belonged to. He was over six feet tall and deceptively lean. His black T-shirt and worn jeans were molded revealingly to a hard muscular body. His wind-whipped hair was black as night, his eyes shielded by intimidating reflector glasses. A coarse stubble accentuated his features, hard features that included an almost imperceptible scar on his upper lip. But Diana saw it clearly enough. All her senses were heightened in that electrified split second. And this man, this dark fierce stranger, was coming straight for her with malice in every taut muscle of his body.

Without a doubt, she had never been in such a vulnerable position in her life. It was a living nightmare, plucked straight out of her brothers' fertile imaginations. Her back pressed into the gate, and her heart lodged in her throat. Not a single coherent thought could be found in her entire brain. Suddenly, instinctively, she raised the can of Mace and pressed the button.

The next moment, her would-be assailant was doubled over, gasping and coughing. He tore off his glasses and dug at his eyes with his fists. "Damn it!" he sputtered. "What did you do? What the hell *was* that?"

Diana stood frozen with a mixture of fear and fascination. She had immobilized him, this terrifying stranger who looked about three times her size. She'd done it!

But even as she was congratulating herself, her brain was telling her to move, to run to her car and speed away before he recovered.

She hadn't taken two steps, however, when the intercom crackled to life. "Yes, may I help you?" came a metallic female voice.

Diana hesitated. Her gaze raced from her car to the man, who was still coughing and rubbing his streaming eyes. Then, aiming the can as if it were a gun, she backed up to the intercom.

"This is Diana White," she said in a badly wavering voice. "I'm the tutor Mrs. Osborne hired for her daughter. Is it possible for you to open the gate? And please, could you hurry?"

Before Diana could receive a reply, the man she thought she was holding at bay crossed the distance that separated them and knocked the can from her grasp. Her mouth opened but she was too terrified to scream. She felt as if she were about to faint. Well, that was probably for the best, she thought through the mists fogging her brain. If she was about to be raped or murdered, she'd rather not be conscious to know about it.

His hands dug into her shoulders—hard powerful hands. She could feel their strength clear down to her toes as they roughly moved her aside.

"Abbie!" he snarled into the intercom, still blinking away tears from his eyes. "I'll take care of the gate."

Diana's breath stopped in her lungs. Her eyes widened, and a feeling of dread far worse than anything she had experienced so far that day crept under her skin.

"Oh, I didn't realize you were there, too," the voice from the intercom answered. "All right. See you in a few minutes, Mr. Prescott."

The first drops of rain began to fall, hissing on the scorched road like the sound of snakes.

CHAPTER TWO

"YOU CAN'T BE!" Diana whispered. "*You're* Mr. Prescott? *You're* the owner of this place?"

He turned on her angrily, still blind with pain. "And *you're* the tutor my sister invited here without consulting me?" His voice resonated like the thunder overhead.

She swallowed hard. Rain was falling steadily now, running in rivulets down his face. "Y-yes. Diana White." She couldn't take her eyes off him, even though looking at him made her heart race. Where had she got the idea that Mr. Prescott was an elderly gentleman? Hadn't the headmistress said he was Mrs. Osborne's uncle?

Or had she merely said "her" uncle, meaning Cissy's, and Diana had misunderstood? Well, whomever he belonged to, this man wasn't a day over thirty-five! He was no gentleman, either, not with that fierce stubble-darkened face and those scruffy clothes!

Yet, even while these thoughts coursed through her mind, he seemed to pull an invisible cloak of dignity around himself, like a man accustomed to authority and respect, rendering his outfit immediately irrelevant.

Her shock over his identity gave way to the horror of what she had just done to him. She glanced at the Mace can lying on the ground and cringed.

"Mr. Prescott, I'm sorry. Are you all right?" She stepped closer, sincerely wanting to help in spite of the irrational sense of danger she felt when she looked at him.

"Of course I'm not all right. What the hell was that, tear gas?"

Diana shrank back. "No, Mace." She watched him lift his constricted face and blink against the cleansing rain. A flash of lightning illuminated his features, making stark his agony and anger. "I really am sorry. I was told that the family wouldn't be here yet, so I didn't have the slightest notion who you were."

"Oh? And is that supposed to be an excuse?" He pulled a handkerchief from his back pocket and wiped his eyes. "Tell me, Miss White, do you make a habit of incapacitating every stranger who has the misfortune to cross your path?"

"No," she offered weakly. "But..." But what? Could she ever come up with an adequate excuse for her reaction? "You frightened me," she said simply, lowering her eyes. Even though his skin looked leather-tough, it was becoming inflamed where the Mace had hit. She could only imagine what would have happened if he hadn't been wearing glasses.

"Good. Then maybe you'll think twice before you go rattling people's gates as if you were trying to break in."

"Break in?" Diana glanced up, wringing her hands. "I wasn't... The gate was locked and the intercom... I didn't think it was working. Listen, this is crazy, Mr. Prescott. Shouldn't we go inside so you can be tended to properly?"

"Wait a minute!" he barked. "Evelyn may have hired you, but that doesn't mean you have to stay hired."

Diana reared back. Whoever or whatever this man was, he certainly didn't mince words.

He wiped his eyes again, then squinted at her with an intensity that made her suspect he was seeing her for the first time. In the downpour, her tank top and shorts had become plastered to her body. She knew it wasn't an outstanding body; in fact, being five foot seven and not exceptionally curvy, her figure had often been described as boyish. Still, it was a frame that wore clothes well, and so far no one had ever said it was inadequate.

She knew she wasn't exactly pretty, either. Her lips were perhaps too thin, and a small bump marred the line of her nose. And unless she was tanned or wore a bit of blush, her cheeks could run to sallow. Yet she knew she had nice eyes, large chocolate-brown eyes with long lashes and lots of expression, and her dark brown hair was thick and healthy. She suspected she let it grow so long—it was now below midback—to compensate for the features that were less than perfect.

Under Mr. Prescott's cold stare, however, her usual confidence wilted. His eyes were hard and judgmental with none of the approval she usually saw in men's eyes.

"Good Lord! How old are you?"

"Nearly t-twenty-six." Her voice was thin and unsure.

One dark eyebrow lifted in surprise. "And where did Evelyn dredge you up?"

"Evelyn. Is that Cissy's mother?"

He barely nodded.

"From F-Fairview." What was happening to her? She didn't ordinarily stammer. "Didn't she tell you?"

"Yes, of course," he said, contradicting himself. His eyes began to stream again, and it was a while before he continued. "But not till yesterday when it was too late for my input. I didn't even know my niece was having trouble with school. So, you're twenty-*five* and from Fairview. I suppose that means you've been teaching all of, what, four years?"

She gulped. "Three."

The look on his face left no doubt about what he thought of her brief career.

With a trembling hand, she wiped the rain from her eyes. "I can assure you, Mr. Prescott, you won't find anyone more hardworking than I am. I'm fully qualified. I've almost finished work on my master's degree. I've received nothing but commendable reviews whenever I've been observed, and..."

She paused in midstream as a wave of resentment coursed through her. Who did this guy think he was, interrogating her in that ridiculously arrogant pose? And what was she doing, thinking she had to justify herself to him?

"Mr. Prescott, I don't see how my credentials can be any of your business. Fairview felt confident enough to recommend me for this position, and your sister was sufficiently satisfied to hire me. In my estimation, that should end the matter. Besides, it's *raining!*"

But his hard-planed face didn't waver from its expression of indurate displeasure. "Don't tell me what *is* and what is *not* my business, Miss White. No one walks into a job here without being interviewed."

Diana's breathing became like a bellows. Never had she met a more insufferable man.

"Now," he went on, feet planted aggressively apart, looking perfectly comfortable in the storm, "I hear that my sister has offered you the rooms over the carriage house."

"That's what I hear, too."

"I hope you realize that if she had asked me, I never would have agreed to this arrangement."

Diana summoned all her dignity. "Then you should have called me. If I had known they weren't available, I would have saved myself a lot of trouble and stayed in Vermont."

His eyes narrowed, dissecting her. "I didn't say they weren't available. I just wanted you to know I'm not happy about the arrangement, that's all, and we should get a few ground rules straight before we proceed."

They stared hard at each other, blinking away the rain, oblivious to the thunder crashing around them. Their hair, nearly identical in color, was now sculpted to their heads. He had such strange eyes, Diana thought. Intelligent sharp eyes. Yet they were hooded, cautious, masking whatever soul lay beneath them. But what arrested her most was the fact those eyes weren't black, as she'd first assumed, given the rest of his coloring, but blue, the blue of the sky on only the best of days. And though she knew perfectly well that eye color had nothing to do with one's character, she couldn't help feeling here was a color that belonged in the eyes, not of this intimidating brute, but of a kind sensitive man.

Suddenly, Diana felt heat rushing to her cheeks for reasons she couldn't fathom. She spun around and looked unseeingly through the gate. "W-what ground rules?"

He cleared his throat officiously. "Well, first of all, the furniture in the carriage house is hardly precious. Still, I expect it to be left in the same condition you find it."

Diana's head swiveled, her wet braid flying out behind her. "What do you think I'm going to do? Gnaw on it? Stuff it into my Toyota and take it back to Vermont?"

In any other man, she would have interpreted the tightened mouth as a suppressed smile, but Mr. Prescott seemed totally unacquainted with humor.

"Secondly," he continued, "while you're on the grounds, please confine your activities to the carriage house. That includes my niece's lessons, too. I'm a busy man, Miss White. Most of the time I'm away on business, but when I am here, I don't want to be bumping into strangers whenever I turn a corner."

Diana could feel her lips disappearing. "I don't have to be told what any polite person would take for granted."

"Fine. Then it's needless to say you're not to bring friends onto the grounds. Friends are to be met in town and left in town."

"I'm from Vermont. I have no friends here. I don't know anyone but your niece." He must be aware of that, she thought. So why burden her with yet another rule, unless he was obsessed with exercising authority?

None of her daggered looks affected him, however. "Another thing, my staff here is old line—loyal, you know? And as long as you're here, I expect you to be the same. Whatever goes on within these walls is not to be gossiped about outside. Do you hear?"

Diana couldn't help smirking at his ridiculous "lord of the manor" attitude.

"Do you hear?" he bellowed.

She snapped, "Yes, sir!" and clicked her heels with military smartness.

The look he gave her was corroding. "I don't care much for insolence, either."

"And when I decide to live under a dictatorship, I'll move to Iran!"

"I'm warning you, your job could depend on it."

"Is that supposed to be a threat?"

"Damn right! And one you'd better heed."

She took a reckless step forward, uncaring that even from her height she had to look up. "Might I remind you that I'm not working for *you*?"

"And might I remind you that you're living on my property?"

"Mr. Prescott?" She could feel her blood racing. "You can stuff your precious property." With that, she stormed off toward her car, her feet squishing noisily in their wet sneakers.

Effortlessly he reached out and caught her upper arm. "One more thing, Miss White," he continued as smooth as ice. "Don't go poking into places you don't belong. I don't like snoops, and I swear I'll personally skin the next maid or gardener—or tutor—who turns out to be a reporter."

Diana gasped. "Mr. Prescott, let's get one thing straight," she said, yanking free of his hold. "I'm not the slightest bit interested in you or your...your estate. I came here to tutor Cissy and that's all. I'm a professional, I always conduct myself in a professional manner, and I don't take kindly to being treated otherwise. Is that clear?" He didn't answer. "Now, are you through?"

Silence spun out for a few long seconds before he replied, "Not yet." He removed a large key from a ring on his belt, then walked to the gate and inserted it into the lock. The gate swung in with a whine.

"Here," he called, casually tossing her the key as if knowing all along she wasn't going to leave. She caught it against her breast. "Lock the gate behind you whenever you go out or come in. That's not just a suggestion. That's a hard and fast order."

She stared at the key and considered flinging it back at him, but suddenly she remembered something, something that had been preying on her thoughts just before his arrival. "Do you let your dogs run free?"

He squinted at her through the rain, a puzzled expression lining his leathery face.

"Your dogs. As in 'Beware of the.'" What an insufferable bully this man was, with his dogs and rules and signs—and that motorcycle! Now she understood why her colleagues had felt so uneasy about her coming here.

He swung one long sinewy leg over the machine and straddled it aggressively. "My last dog died three years ago."

He kicked the bike into thundering life. "Miss White!" he called over the roar.

"Yes-s-s, what is it *now?*"

His mysterious blue eyes swept over her slowly, missing nothing. "Welcome to Cliff Haven." Then he went streaking through the gate, leaving her behind trying to catch her breath.

DIANA DROVE HER CAR through the gate, stopped, got out and locked the gate, just as Mr. Prescott had instructed. She was still trembling through every inch of her body.

The long driveway opened out onto a wide cobbled courtyard in front of the main house. Perhaps in fair weather she would feel better about it, but at the moment it seemed such a forbidding place.

Diana stopped her car in the middle of this dismal rain-pounded square and glanced around. Mr. Prescott's motorcycle was parked beneath the portico, but he himself had disappeared. To her right stood a smaller two-story stone structure she assumed was the carriage house. Having abandoned her, did Mr. Prescott expect her to let herself in?

Just then, the front door opened, and a tall dark-haired woman in a plastic raincoat came crinkling out. She was built like a rampart, but as she got closer, Diana realized she was old. Her face was mapped with creases, and her hair had obviously been dyed. Still, she was smiling, and the harshness of her hair did not diminish the softness in her eyes.

"Hello!" It was the same voice Diana had heard over the intercom. "Ungodly weather to be arriving in. The garage doors are open. Go park inside, and I'll meet you there."

Diana headed into one of the wide stalls. She switched off the engine and quickly surveyed her surroundings. There were none of the mile-long limousines she'd expected, just an old truck and a sporty-looking sedan.

The elderly woman came lumbering through the doorway, and Diana got out of her car, wishing her legs weren't still so wobbly.

"I'm Mrs. Burns, the housekeeper. But call me Abbie, or I'll get very cross with you."

"Diana White." She held out her hand, and the woman grasped it warmly in both of hers.

"What a treat to have you with us this summer!" Though she looked fairly strong, Diana noticed her head shook with a slight palsy. "Oh, child, you're soaked to the skin."

Diana felt her cheeks warming. "I—I met Mr. Prescott at the gate, and we talked for a while."

"Yes, I know." The humor left the housekeeper's eyes, making Diana wonder if she'd overheard any of the ruckus through the intercom. "If you don't mind my asking, what did you do to the poor devil? He came into the house in a terrible state. He hollered that you were here and I was to get myself outside to meet you. Then he tore straight up the stairs and slammed shut his bedroom door."

"I—I sprayed him with Mace," she offered softly.

The old woman's eyes narrowed. "You what?"

"I sprayed him. With Mace. You see, I was at the gate when he came up out of nowhere. He scared the life out of me, so..."

"You sprayed him."

Diana nodded, wondering if the housekeeper was framing a stiff tongue-lashing, being "old line" and "loyal," as Mr. Prescott had phrased it.

But then a smile broke over Abbie's frown. "Well, good for you. That's what he deserves for going around looking like a hooligan and driving that hooligan machine."

Diana relaxed a little. "The effects should wear off soon, but maybe somebody should tend to him."

Abbie waved dismissively. "David could be dying and he wouldn't let anyone tend to him."

David. So his name was David.

"Abbie, I hate to pry, but is he always so... odd?"

The housekeeper seemed to be weighing her reply. "He's just been cooped up with his accountants for the past two weeks. The end of the fiscal year, you know. He's unwinding." Then she snorted. "Big deal! He comes here, doesn't say anything worth a plug nickel, doesn't do anything but read and walk back and forth to the seawall—and ride that infernal machine. Then he goes back to work all rested, as if he's been on a cruise to the Bahamas. I tell you, sometimes he makes me so mad..." Her face screwed up with exasperation. "Maybe I should get myself some Mace, too, and then when I want to get his attention, all I'll have to do is squirt." Suddenly she laughed and Diana couldn't help joining in. "C'mon. Let's take your bags upstairs and get you settled. And don't you give another thought to young David. He'll get over your Mace. He's gotten over worse."

Diana followed Abbie up a flight of narrow stone stairs that hugged the outside of the building. The apartment smelled musty, having been closed up for some time, but it was spacious and comfortably furnished in a delightful jumble of late Victoriana and Art Deco. It consisted of a living-dining area, a kitchen and a bedroom.

"This is really cute." Diana smiled, setting down her bag.

"I've always liked it, too. My husband and I lived here ourselves when we first came to work for the Prescotts."

Diana didn't have to ask. She knew by the woman's expression that Mr. Burns was deceased.

"Oh, my, but these windows are dirty!" Abbie cried, lifting aside the lace curtain. "I used to do them twice a year, but the big house is about all I can handle these days."

"Surely you don't take care of the whole place yourself?"

"In the off-season I do," she asserted proudly. "It isn't hard. Nobody's here to muss the place, except David once in a while, but he comes and goes like a ghost. Doesn't even leave laundry."

"Still, the house is enormous!"

"Eighteen rooms!" She paused and studied Diana's expression. "Oh, I know what you're thinking. You're thinking Abbie's getting too old to take care of the house the way she used to." Her head was shaking more noticeably now. "Well, maybe. I'll turn seventy-five two weeks from next Friday. But I'm not ready to be put out to pasture yet."

Diana gazed out the window toward the ivy-bearded mansion across the way. "I'm sure you're very capable," she murmured, wondering if there was someone in the old woman's life who didn't think she was.

They carried her bags into the bedroom, then explored the kitchen until Diana was familiar with the quirky old appliances. When she opened the refrigerator to turn it on, her eyes widened. Not only was it already cold, but someone had stocked it with food.

"I didn't think you'd feel up to going shopping after such a long drive."

Diana felt a rush of affection for the old woman, especially after just having met the ogre she worked for. "Thanks, Abbie," she said, giving her arm a friendly squeeze.

"If it was up to me, I'd have you over to the house for your meals, but . . ." She lifted her shoulders in an eloquent shrug.

"That's okay. I understand."

Abbie looked at her thoughtfully, nodding to some inner voice. "Yep, Mace. That's what we all need." And they both laughed again.

"Oh, before you go..." Diana said. "Has Mrs. Osborne arrived, by any chance?"

"No. She'll be coming in tomorrow. Which reminds me, tell me about our little Celia. What's she done to bring you here?"

"She failed English this year."

Abbie wagged her head. "Now, why'd she go and do a foolish thing like that?"

"I've been wondering about it myself." Diana hesitated. "Maybe she was in love."

"Maybe," Abbie murmured doubtfully.

Diana glanced up sharply. "What do *you* think her problem was?"

The woman's gaze seemed to turn inward. "The poor child probably couldn't study for wondering what's to become of... of her summers after her uncle's gone and sold this place."

"Mr. Prescott is going to sell Cliff Haven?"

Abbie nodded indignantly. "After it's been in the family for four generations, too."

Diana felt the imprudent stirrings of concern and she paused. But only for a moment. "Abbie, how long have you worked here?"

"Oh, let's see. It'll be fifty-seven years come October."

Diana's eyes snapped wide open.

"I've known them all, even Zeke, the one who built the place. But he was real old, died the year after I came. Then Kate and Justin took over. David's grandparents." Abbie's eyes brightened. "Those were grand days! We had a staff of twenty people then, even though it was the depression. Parties on weekends, all the bedrooms full of guests."

"Sounds exciting."

"Oh, it was. Things got a little quieter during the last reign," she continued, fondly mocking a family she obviously loved. "There were still parties, but Miss Loretta was a lady," she pronounced with significant dignity.

"David's mother?"

Abbie nodded. "She was the most beautiful woman in all society. I used to tell my Andrew she had royal blood in her. She and Walter made a dashing couple. He was very handsome, too. Like all the Prescotts, don't you think?"

Diana was confused by the heat flushing her face. She had to admit that the Prescott she'd just met had, well, riveting looks. But *handsome?*

"How about the present reign? What are they like?"

"They? Why, there's only David and Evelyn now."

"David never married?" Diana blushed harder, hearing the curiosity that had unwittingly slipped into her tone.

"No." Abbie answered simply, yet almost evasively, Diana thought.

"So, not much goes on here anymore?"

"No. They...they have their lives...." Abbie shuffled to the door. Diana followed, lost in speculation.

"Now, listen, child. If you need anything, don't hesitate to come over to the house and give a holler."

"Thank you," Diana said, though she had no intention of going anywhere near the house while David Prescott was in it. "And you be careful on those wet stairs."

As soon as the housekeeper was gone, Diana put her mind to settling in. It was a cute little place, a place that would provide peace and solitude for nearly two months. And she would be hanged before she'd let anyone turn it into a prison!

CHAPTER THREE

DIANA AWOKE to the crashing of waves, the caw of gulls, the smell of wet grass and pungent salt air. She blinked open her eyes and then remembered. She was in Newport.

She slipped out of bed and went to the window. The sun was shining brightly, turning the lingering beads of rain on her screen into jewels. She leaned on the sill and let all the new sights and sounds and smells wash over her. This morning she was definitely glad she'd come to Newport.

She only wished she felt more rested. Unfortunately, she'd tossed and turned for too many hours. David Prescott seemed to be sitting there all night long, right behind her eyes, reminding her she was not welcome here.

She'd tried to feel sorry for him. Her unexpected and undoubtedly painful attack had given him every reason to be angry. But nothing she told herself worked. She could only continue to see him as a cold insulting brute!

The best thing, she decided, was simply to forget him. He had nothing to do with her duties here. Besides, he'd probably be leaving on one of his business trips soon, and with any luck, she'd never run into him again.

She left the window and padded out to the kitchen to make herself some coffee. She wished she could call Skip and tell him she'd arrived safely, but she knew from her search last night that the carriage house had no phone.

Feeling rather cut off from the outside world, she went into the bathroom and turned on the shower. At least she had hot water!

By ten o'clock, she had her hair blow-dried and arranged in a neat chignon. She'd applied her makeup lightly but carefully, and slipped on a proper little dress of cream-colored linen. She'd even struggled into nylons. Nervously, she decided she was as ready for the day as she would ever be. Now she could only hope that Mrs. Osborne wasn't a female version of her overbearing brother!

She settled into a chair overlooking the courtyard and opened her copy of *Moby Dick,* the first novel she and Cissy would be tackling. But after reading the same passage three times, she tossed the book aside. She longed to get outside and take an exploratory walk around the grounds. She longed to breathe the fresh salt air. But, considering the narrow parameters Mr. Prescott had set for her, she immediately dismissed the idea.

Damn the man and his stupid rules! And damn him doubly for continually intruding on her thoughts after she'd vowed to ignore him.

Well, he certainly couldn't object to her making a simple call home, she thought, rising determinedly from her chair.

Nevertheless, her legs felt like rubber as she crossed the courtyard. After taking a deep calming breath, she lifted the brass door-knocker and let it fall.

"Yes?" It was Mr. Prescott, sharp and impatient. Diana glanced up and around the shadows of the portico, wondering where his voice was coming from. "Yes, what do you want, Miss White?"

"Sorry to disturb you, Mr. Prescott." She felt a bit like Dorothy standing before the gates of Oz. "Mr. Prescott, may I use your phone for a quick call home?" She wondered if he could hear the hammering of her heart.

"Yes, yes." Abruptly he cut their connection. Diana stared at the door uncertainly. Was he coming to meet her? Was he sending someone else? The next moment, the intercom hummed back into life. "Well, are you going to stand there all day? Let yourself in, Miss White." Then he was gone again.

She opened the heavy door and inched into the cool marble-floored foyer. His voice drifted from a room to her left. The door was open. She peeked in. A library.

He was pacing across a red Persian rug, a phone to his ear. Lines like quotation marks furrowed his brow. "If you can bring the cost down to two dollars a unit, we'll take the lot. Otherwise, I'm afraid we'll have to look elsewhere."

When he noticed Diana, his pacing stopped, and just for a moment he looked a bit off balance. She supposed she looked different today—efficient, professional, maybe even pretty.

But if *her* appearance surprised him, *his* completely bowled her over. She knew she was staring but she couldn't stop. It was amazing what a shower and a shave could do for a man. His hair was brushed back in a semblance of civility, and in place of yesterday's scruffy clothes, he now wore a blue cotton sweater and pleated white trousers, looking for all the world as if he'd just stepped out of a glossy yachting magazine.

Yet, in spite of this new image, she realized he still made her shiver with an intimation of danger. She felt an almost physical release as he returned his attention to his phone conversation.

"Good. My representative will meet with you next Thursday then . . . Nice talking to you, too." He put the phone down on the desk and stared at it for a moment, lost in thought.

"Mr. Pres—"

"Just a moment." He lifted the receiver again and punched out a number. Diana huffed and decided to sit down.

"Max. Hi. David..."

Diana's attention shifted to his face. Lean, determined, the face of a winner. It was also the face of someone you wouldn't want to cross.

"I'm sending Lou out to Stuttgart next week, but I want you to go with him... Exactly. That factory doesn't have a chance unless we get those parts on our terms." He was pacing nervously again although his voice still ran smooth and strong. "Sure enough. See you Monday." He put down the phone and finally turned to Diana, though it was a moment before his thoughts seemed to catch up to him.

She rose from her seat. "I'm really sorry to disturb you, but I promised my brother I'd call him when I got here."

He went around his cluttered desk and collapsed into the cracked leather chair behind it. His stare was unnerving. Cool, judgmental. Nevertheless Diana felt her cheeks warming uncomfortably. "Sure. But make it brief. My sister should be here any minute."

She walked to the desk and picked up the receiver, glancing meaningfully in his direction, but evidently he had no intention of leaving the room. Instead, he picked up a newspaper, the *Sunday New York Times,* and rustled open the business section. For a person so hung up on privacy, he certainly didn't think much about hers.

"Hi, Skip? It's me... Yes, I got here just fine..."

As she talked, she noticed David's eyes lift from the paper occasionally to flick over her, and she was dismayed to realize that her own eyes were fixed on him each time. But for the life of her, she still couldn't stop staring. Not that he was a man she could actually be attracted to. A man had to be warm, sensitive, have a sense of humor. And as far as she could see, David Prescott possessed none of these qualities. But she had to admit Abbie was right. He really was handsome. Objectively speaking, of course.

She could hear voices over the phone. "Is that Dan and Sylvia? Are you people heading out to church together?... I won't keep you, then... Oh, is Robin there, too?... Yes, put her on... Hi, Robin. How's my punkin today?"

Over the rim of the paper, she noticed Mr. Prescott's face screw up with disgust. Well, excuse *me!* Did he think that every call a person made had to determine the fate of whole factories? Again his eyes met hers, seemingly drawn by her thinking about him. Disturbingly blue, they became like physical prods, hurrying her conversation along.

Luckily, Skip came back on the line then and asked for a number where she could be reached. She began to read it off the phone, only to have a hand come down over it swiftly.

"Skip, don't call here. I'll call you... Yes, I've got to go, too."

She almost slammed down the receiver. "Thank you," she said tightly.

"That's an unlisted number, Miss White." He sat back, folded the newspaper and flung it onto a nearby window seat. Next to it, like alien visitors from the future, stood a new fax machine and a large computer. "I think you and I ought to have another talk," he said.

Diana felt her palms go clammy. She was Dorothy again, about to confront the fire and roar of the Great Oz. But she would *not* let him know that.

"Sure." She pulled a chair closer and sat before he could invite her to. She lifted her chin confidently, and when he opened his mouth to speak, she beat him to it. "I'm glad to see you suffered no lasting effects from our meeting yesterday." His lips parted again, but again she interrupted. "I'm sorry. It was a terrible thing to do, but I was *so* nervous about your watchdogs..."

"Mace has no effect on dogs," he finally slipped in.

"It doesn't? Oh." That slowed her momentum.

"I'm not condemning you for carrying Mace, Miss White. A person can never be too cautious. Just keep it away from me. Okay?"

Diana waited to see if he would apologize in turn. But obviously he didn't see anything wrong with his abrasiveness yesterday. "Is there anything else you wanted to talk about?" She managed a small smile.

"Uh, yes," he said vaguely, sounding a bit like someone who's lost his train of thought. "I'd like to know how long this tutoring of yours is going to take."

"About eight weeks."

"That long? Hmm. Can it be hurried up a bit?"

Diana was about to say maybe. "No."

"Hmm." He touched his fingertips together as he rocked back and forth in the creaking old chair, thinking. It was then that Diana noticed the papers on his desk. They looked familiar. It was downright uncanny but...yes, they *were*. They were her records! Transcripts of grades, applications, letters of recommendation, department reviews. Within seconds, her blood was roiling. Where did he get them? Who was this man that he *could* get them?

Before she could say anything, however, two cars pulled into the courtyard.

"That's probably my sister now."

Diana rose from her chair uncertainly. "Are you going out to meet her?"

"No. I have a few more calls to make."

So she'd have to go out and introduce herself. She was sure her eyes were spitting fire by now, but he merely reached for the phone and began to dial—telling her in his inimitable way that she was dismissed.

By the time she reached the portico, she'd managed to swallow her anger. Car doors were already opening and people were piling out. Diana froze in her tracks. *That* was not the Cissy Osborne she remembered. The Cissy she knew opted for neat preppy outfits with a wholesome outdoorsy look. The Cissy she knew smiled interminably and wore her shiny brown hair in a bouncy bob. But the girl slouching out of the station wagon down there in the courtyard made Diana want to cry.

She'd clipped her hair scalp-close over one ear and shaved a lightning bolt into it. The other side, left chin-length, was streaked with green dye. Her face was powdered white, her lips painted stark red, and she was wearing a skintight tube top and jeans torn in all the most unlikely places. It wasn't so much the outfit that got to Diana. She'd seen the punk look before, even at Fairview. It was just that it seemed such a drastic change for Cissy.

"Hi, Cissy. Good to see you again." Diana approached the girl with a smile, determined to hide her reaction.

Cissy's eyes darted up and back to the ground. "Hi, Miss White." A pink wash of embarrassment shone through her ghostly makeup. Diana's heart went out to her. Something was definitely wrong.

"Miss White?"

Diana turned reluctantly toward the voice. A thin dark-haired woman was holding out her hand. "I'm Evelyn Osborne, Cissy's mother."

"Oh. Pleased to meet you."

"Have you been here long?"

"I just got here yesterday."

"Well, I'm certainly glad you agreed to join us this summer. It's a real break for Cissy." It was impossible not to notice the helpless look the woman cast in her daughter's direction. "I'm pleased we managed to get someone from Fairview, too. I have a high regard for all the instructors there. I went there myself when I was a girl."

"Which was only a couple of years ago, I'll have you know," said a robust middle-aged man unlocking the back of the station wagon.

Evelyn laughed, easing the worry lines from her thin face. "Miss White, this is Emmet Thorndike. He was kind enough to make the trip with us from New York."

Diana shook his hand. He was handsome, with smiling green eyes and a personality that seemed cheerful and relaxed. He had red hair, peppered with gray, and wore a plaid shirt and bright green golf pants—an oddball, she decided, among all these dark gloomy people.

A moment later, the courtyard was full of activity. Two extra maids, up from New York for the summer, had emerged from the second car, and Abbie had come out of the house, accompanied by a short gnarled man of about sixty who Diana soon learned was the caretaker, James. Then they were all hugging each other and shaking hands and saying how good it was to be back at Cliff Haven.

All but David Prescott, that is. He preferred to stay inside. Making business calls. On Sunday morning. What could his heart be made of? she wondered. Though she'd accepted this job partly to get away from her overbearing brothers, now she couldn't help thinking of them—and how much they could teach Mr. Prescott about simple courtesy.

"Have you met my brother yet?"

Aware that she'd been gazing at the library window, she turned in time to notice Mrs. Osborne swallow uncomfortably.

"Uh, yes." That's all she could say without revealing her own discomfort. "Mrs. Osborne, I was wondering," she went on quickly, "if it would be all right if I had a phone installed."

"Oh, of course." But then the woman paused. "I suppose I should clear it with David first."

Diana frowned. It seemed even Mrs. Osborne had to get his permission before making the simplest of decisions.

The trunk lid was lifted and soon everyone was pitching in to unload luggage. "When would you like me to start Cissy's lessons?" Diana asked, gripping the handle of a large case with Cissy's name on it.

"Let's see, tomorrow's the Fourth of July. Tuesday? Is that convenient for you?" Although Mrs. Osborne resembled her brother physically, she had none of his aloofness or acerbity. On the contrary, she seemed eager to please, insecure, even nervous at times, causing Diana to wonder if this house was filled with nothing but problems and enigmas.

"Tuesday's fine with me. Okay, Cissy? Nine a.m., up in my apartment?"

"Sure." The girl tried to smile but only managed to look mildly nauseated.

Together, Diana and her young pupil carried the case up the steps. At the front door, she hesitated. Should she go in? Did she have his majesty's okay? Immediately, she realized how absurd the thought was. Why shouldn't she go in? How could she not? Even Abbie was working. Besides, she wanted to spend a little time with Cissy, to establish a bond as soon as possible. Diana wasn't sure what was bothering the girl, but she did know she wanted to help.

David Prescott came to the library door as they were passing, and her heart began pounding unnaturally.

"Hey, Uncle David." Diana was amazed to see Cissy smile.

"Hey, kid." She was equally amazed that he didn't comment on his niece's hair. But then she realized he probably hadn't even noticed it. His eyes hadn't left Diana for a second.

She lifted her chin and walked on with as much dignity as she could muster, although her knees were dangerously weak. She wished she knew why she was reacting this way; it was so unlike her....

Cissy led her across the marbled foyer and into an enormous sitting room. Tall French doors at the opposite end opened onto a terrace. In the adjacent dining room, Diana caught a glimpse of a gleaming cherrywood table that could easily accommodate a party of twenty guests, and beyond that . . . a billiard room? In the other direction was a music room, oval in shape and half glassed-in by ornately beveled windows. Sunlight, caught in their facets, danced upon a grand piano and across the parquet floor.

The staircase was to the right of the sitting room. It was a dramatic marble affair, curving up to a horseshoe balcony that overhung the room below. Off the balcony were the bedrooms, with their pale Aubusson rugs, mantels shipped from castles in Europe, wall silks from France, and adjoining baths carved out of marble.

Cliff Haven was little short of fabulous. It was the definitive summer place, built for guests, meant for entertaining. Yet, as Diana walked its tapestry-hung halls, she got the oddest feeling she was wandering through a lifeless shrine to the past. The antiques, though quite valuable, she was sure, were a jumble of differing styles. The wall coverings and draperies looked dingy and worn. She felt sorry for the old place. Apparently its owner couldn't have cared less about it, and hadn't for quite some time.

"This is my room," Cissy finally announced with a sigh of boredom.

"How beautiful, Cissy!"

"It used to be my mother's when she was young. It's always been 'the girl's room,'" she drawled with mocking gravity as they lowered the case. Finally free of her burden, Cissy kicked off her sandals and plunked herself down on the bed.

Diana walked to a window and gazed out on the back lawn. The grass was vibrantly green after yesterday's rain, and the gardens were blooming. There was a gazebo down by the seawall, a three-tiered fountain in the center, though she suspected it was broken, and way to the left, a boarded-up stable. Beyond all this was the ocean, glittering like endless silver dust. Whether she liked Cliff Haven or not, Diana had to admit it was worth a fortune for its view alone. She turned. Voices drifted from other rooms along the corridor. Abbie's voice. Evelyn Osborne's.

"Your mother's very nice," she commented casually.

Cissy just shrugged. "What do you think of David?"

Diana felt her pulse jump again, as it always did when he was mentioned. "I don't think your mother cleared my coming here with him."

"Why? Did he give you a hard time?"

"Slightly."

"Don't take it personally." Cissy paused, eyes lost to inner thoughts. "And don't be upset with my mother. She didn't tell him about you till the last minute because she didn't want to give him the chance to veto you. And he most likely would have, too. He doesn't like anybody but us staying here, and she knew I absolutely had to get tutored this summer. It took a lot for her to do that." Cissy pulled a tissue from a dispenser on her nightstand and began to rub off her makeup.

Diana returned to gazing out the window, her frown deepening. "Who's Emmet Thorndike?"

After a heavy pause, "Nobody."

Diana swiveled around, one eyebrow arched in a stern question mark.

"He's the president of one of my uncle's plants."

"Is that all?"

Cissy's lips pressed into a hard bloodless line. "Yes," she said, and Diana knew that was not all. An inner voice, which sounded remarkably like Mr. Prescott's, reminded her not to go prying where she didn't belong, and yet her instincts told her the time was right. Besides, if it concerned Cissy's well-being, she *did* belong.

"Is he dating your mother?"

Cissy snorted contemptuously.

"I see. And you don't approve?"

"At their age? It's ridiculous."

"It must be difficult. You've had your mother all to yourself for the past eight years."

Cissy averted her peevish eyes. "I don't really care, Miss White."

"Well, hang in. Things'll work out." Diana knew she'd pressed far enough. For now, anyway. "I should be going. You must have a lot to do, first day here and all." She crossed the room to check the time on a porcelain clock on the fireplace mantel. "You'll be wanting to have lunch soon, too." She was about to turn away when she spotted a small framed photograph beside the clock. She picked it up before any inner voice could warn her not to.

"Cissy, who are these children? Is this your mother and David?"

The girl glanced over. "Uh-huh. Walter, too. My mother's other brother."

Diana looked closer. She hadn't realized there *was* another brother. The three youngsters, all with similar features and the same dark hair, were sitting on a blanket in bathing suits. Evelyn was the oldest, a teenager at the time.

As usual, David was scowling. Even at the age of ten or eleven, he looked haughty and detached. Beside him was the younger boy, slim and tanned and brightly smiling, one arm linked affectionately through his sullen older brother's, the other wrapped around the neck of a huge wet Labrador. Sunlight streaked his raven-smooth hair and gleamed within his clear trusting eyes.

"Your Uncle Walter sure was cute."

"Walter?" Cissy hopped off the bed.

"Mm. This adorable child with his arm around the dog."

Cissy threw back her head and hooted with laughter. "Miss White, that isn't Walter."

"It isn't?" Then color flamed in Diana's cheeks. She felt it creep right up to her scalp.

Cissy stared at her with an awkward quivering smile, and perhaps thinking she had dealt her tutor's composure a mortal blow, she also blushed and began to stammer. "H-he's the youngest, David is. We don't see Uncle Walter anymore. Not since he and David... I mean... He lives in Pennsylvania with Aunt Glenda and their two boys. I don't know them. We don't visit. Uncle David and Glenda..."

Diana looked up, sharply curious, but Cissy had gone silent, her eyes fixed on a point somewhere over Diana's shoulder.

On a sudden wave of dread, Diana spun around. There stood David Prescott, looming on the threshold like a huge dark storm about to break.

"I'm sorry," she whispered, not knowing what she had done, only that something was terribly wrong. Unsteadily, she placed the frame back on the mantel.

"What's up, Uncle David?" Cissy sounded unnaturally cheerful.

But he didn't answer. He just went on glaring at Diana until she thought she would die.

"Well, if that's all I can help with, Cissy..." She took a step toward the hall.

"Where are you going, Miss White?"

"I'm sorry. I have to go. I... There are errands I have to run in the city. Excuse me," she said, her voice growing fainter. But David Prescott refused to move. She glanced up, her eyes defenseless against his.

Was this really the same person she had just seen in the photograph? Were these the same eyes that had once looked out on the world with such openness and love? At the moment they looked more like the eyes of an animal—an animal who has been whipped until it's grown irrevocably mean.

"Please," she begged weakly.

After what seemed an eternity, he stepped aside. She was barely down the stairs before tears flooded her vision.

CHAPTER FOUR

DIANA CLOSED THE DOOR of her apartment and turned the lock. She told herself she wasn't going to cry, but the tears kept coming. She felt miserable, and the worst part was she didn't have the foggiest idea why. David Prescott hadn't said a word. It was only that she'd never seen a look like that before, so angry, so pained. What had she done?

True, he'd told her to confine her activities to the carriage house, and just this morning she'd used his phone, met his family and staff, and gone up to one of the bedrooms. But did actions as ordinary as these really warrant such a reaction?

No, intuition told her it had more to do with that photograph. Had she stumbled across a family skeleton? The estranged brother perhaps? What had David done to the poor guy?

Diana blew her nose, still denying that she was crying. Something was definitely rotten in this state of Denmark, and if she had any sense at all, she would let it lie. Not only was it none of her business, but she had enough problems of her own.

She picked up her handbag, checked her appearance in a mirror by the door and headed down the stairs. The time was ripe for getting away and doing some sightseeing. With any luck everyone would be asleep when she returned.

She backed her car out of the garage and turned it around in the courtyard. But just as she was about to head down the drive, the front door of the main house opened and David Prescott stepped out. Diana's lungs felt on fire. He looked directly at her as he descended the stairs. She had the oddest feeling he wanted to speak to her.

Well, David Prescott could go straight to hell. She'd had enough of him for one day. She stepped on the gas so hard her tires squealed and left a black scar on the bricks.

FOR HOURS THAT AFTERNOON Diana walked the narrow streets of the harbor district, admiring the beautifully restored homes of the colonial era. And when she tired of that, she wandered down America's Cup Avenue to the wharves, lined with countless little shops. In spite of the emotional turmoil that had driven her here, she realized she was famished. She found a cheerful outdoor café where she ordered a hamburger and listened to a trio of country fiddlers.

Feeling infinitely better, she continued on her way. She ended up buying a bag of peach potpourri to chase away the mustiness at the carriage house, five plants because the place was in dire need of something green and alive, and a bag of exotically flavored jelly beans simply because she couldn't resist them.

Then, since she still wasn't ready to face Cliff Haven again, she drove to the Bellevue Avenue area in search of The Breakers, the seventy-two-room Vanderbilt mansion styled after an Italian palazzo. When that tour ended, she zipped down the road and visited Rosecliff, a replica of the Grand Trianon at Versailles.

Somehow, she managed to stay out till nearly eleven o'clock, but she could forestall the inevitable no longer.

How dark Cliff Haven was after the bustle of the harbor! Nothing stirred. Only the ocean, rushing and retreating over the rocky shore below the cliff.

Diana washed quickly and settled into bed with *Moby Dick*. Totally exhausted from her busy day, she fell asleep with her light still on. But in the middle of the night she awoke again. She sat up, suddenly fully alert and listening. Her travel alarm read two forty-five.

She slipped out of bed and made herself a cup of hot milk, but it did little to calm her restlessness. She wandered to the window and stared at the main house sleeping across the way. The next minute, she tied on her sneakers, threw a sweater over her nightgown and slipped out the door. She glanced at the house once again and frowned, remembering the unreasonable emotions its owner had aroused in her that day. He was an autocrat, that's what he was. And autocracy was meant to be defied!

She found her way around the carriage house and crossed the back lawn. Before long she reached the seawall. It was a beautiful soft night. Below her, waves were rolling in, just a glimmer of stars sparkling over their foam.

And then her heart stopped. She clutched the wall and leaned forward, squinting. No, her eyes were not deceiving her. There really was someone out there.

A stairway led from the lawn, down the cliff to a pier of some sort, and at the end of that pier, with dark waves surging all around, stood a solitary man. From his size and build, it was unmistakably David Prescott.

What in heaven's name was he doing out there at three in the morning, gazing at the ocean and looking so... so lost? Was he communing with the night? Pining for lost love? Was he plotting some ungodly business takeover? What was going on inside that head, behind those gorgeous frightening blue eyes?

Diana knew she should get back to the carriage house. He would be angry if he discovered her wandering the grounds. Besides, he wasn't worth her curiosity. He was nothing but a . . . a businessman, an ill-mannered bad-tempered one at that.

But still she lingered, drawn to watching him as if he were a mystery just beginning to unfold. In fact, she watched until David himself turned and began to tread up the pier. And if she went back to her bed imagining there was more to him than met the eye, well, that was an indulgence she supposed she could tolerate for one night.

EARLY THE NEXT MORNING Diana heard movement in the garage below. She was already dressed and busy, even though it was a holiday. The carriage house was passably clean, but not as fresh as she would have liked it, and she'd decided to spend the day scrubbing—and trying not to think about the Fourth of July cookout back home, or the annual softball game, or the family from whom she was supposedly here to declare her independence.

Again the noise. Mildly curious, she put down her scrub brush and went to the window. The blue sedan was pulling out of the garage. It stopped at the main house and James got out to lift the hood. At the same time David Prescott appeared, briefcase in hand. He was wearing a dark suit, white shirt and conservative navy tie. Even from a distance, Diana was impressed. The suit hugged his lean powerful body with subtle sensuality even while presenting the most proper business form.

Could this really be the same man who had roared up on a Harley just two days before? she wondered. She wished she weren't so intrigued, but he was such a study in contradictions.

When she realized he was staring up at the carriage house, she jumped back from the window, her heart lodged in her throat.

Get back to work, you idiot! she told herself. She resumed washing the floor, but it wasn't long before she was peeking over the sill again.

He was pacing the courtyard while the caretaker tinkered with the engine. He looked preoccupied, one hand occasionally combing through his hair. Suddenly he paused and Diana's heartbeat seemed to pause along with him. Then, as if powered by some momentous decision, he loped toward her stairs. In less than a second, it seemed, he was at the door, peering down at her through the screen. She got up and wiped her hands on her shorts. She couldn't find her voice as she opened the door.

And for a while it seemed neither could he.

His high cheekbones and straight, perfectly arrogant nose were brushed-stroked with sun, and he exuded a clean masculine fragrance that momentarily derailed her train of thought.

"Good morning," he finally said.

The only reply she could muster was a confused nod.

"I just came over to see if everything was all right here. For my niece's lessons, I mean."

"Yes, fine." She regained enough presence of mind to remember to scowl.

He nodded with a serious businesslike economy. At the same time, though, she was aware of his eyes traveling over her with an interest she found disturbing, taking in her long loosely tied hair, the heightened color of her cheeks, the snug fit of her cutoffs.

"Well, if there's anything you need..."

"No, nothing."

His gaze finally released her and roamed to the curtainless windows, over the stacked furniture and new plants, and back down to the pail of sudsy water at her feet. For a moment, Diana felt sure he was going to sail into her for up-ending the place. His eyes narrowed and he shook his head slightly as if in exasperation. But that was all.

Diana didn't know what to say, and her speechlessness confused her. Why couldn't she just boot the man down the stairs as he deserved, instead of standing here feeling self-conscious and uncomfortable and so very *aware* of him? She didn't understand this one bit. She thoroughly disliked him, and he disliked her. So why was she feeling these stirrings of femininity under his gaze? This was the wrong time, the wrong place and he was most definitely the wrong man.

"The car's all set, Mr. Prescott," the caretaker called.

"Be right down." He turned back to Diana and the hardness that usually rendered his face unreadable seemed to drop for a second. A look that resembled frustration troubled his eyes. "I also came over to say—"

"Your plane's leaving in fifteen minutes. Really, sir, we've got to hurry."

"Damn!" she thought he whispered. He raked Diana's features with a thoroughness that left her slightly breathless. "Well, take care. And stay out of trouble while I'm gone, hm?"

Diana nodded, blinking at him with wide incredulous brown eyes. His appearance was hard enough to handle this early on a Monday morning, but this sudden overture of . . . of what? Why *was* he here? she wondered.

He said nothing more. He simply turned and hurried down the stairs, moving with a masculine sensuality that finally made her realize why he'd frightened her so much.

DIANA WAS HANGING curtains over a makeshift line in the bathroom when Evelyn Osborne knocked on her door.

"What *are* you doing?" the older woman exclaimed.

"Oh, hi." Diana came out to the front room. "I hope you don't mind."

"No, of course not. But you should have said something if you didn't find the place adequate."

"Oh, but I did. I do." Diana tugged the old vacuum cleaner aside. "I get a kick out of cleaning, that's all. Not everyday drudge cleaning, mind you, but I love to turn a house inside out occasionally. Come in."

"Thanks. I won't be long. I just came to ask if you'd like to watch the Bristol Parade with us. Emmet is sailing us over."

Diana guessed she looked confused.

"Bristol isn't far, but the traffic's horrendous on the Fourth. Going by boat is the fastest way to travel. Come on, Diana. It's a fabulous parade, the oldest in the country. It takes hours and hours to watch. Besides, you can't spend the holiday cleaning."

Diana began to smile. She loved parades. So much for not having anything in common with "wealthy society people."

"I'd love to. Let me change."

"Great. Mind if I stay? There's something else I'd like to talk about. Go ahead. I'll talk through the door."

Diana hurried to her room, intrigued.

"I heard about your little melee with my brother at the gate."

Through the door, Diana heard the woman's soft chuckle. "It wasn't funny, Mrs. Osborne."

"No, I don't suppose it was. If there's anything David can't abide it's feeling vulnerable. And please, call me Evelyn."

Diana slipped on a corn-yellow blouse and a pair of matching trousers. "He's a hard person to understand, Mrs. —Evelyn."

"That's for sure! In an article *Fortune* did a few years ago, he was described as industry's lone hawk, King Midas, a white knight with an assassin's stare..." She paused and chuckled. "His inscrutability drives people batty, especially reporters searching for metaphors. And his competitors."

Diana opened the door. "Evelyn, something tells me he wouldn't approve of our talking about him."

"You're right again. There isn't much he values more than his privacy. But I don't want you going through the summer hating him, or misunderstanding, and that's why I'm going to talk anyway."

"What's to misunderstand?" Diana picked up a brush and hastily pulled it through her hair.

"Everything, if you don't really know David." Evelyn sighed and walked to the window. "He wasn't always so difficult, Diana. Believe it or not, he was once a pretty terrific kid—cheerful, loving, certainly the smartest of us three. I have another brother, you know," she admitted hesitantly. "Walter."

"Yes. Cissy mentioned him briefly." Diana put down the brush and left her room to come sit on the couch.

"Mm. David was so bright, always taking things apart to see how they worked, always inventing things..." She sighed as if under the weight of too many memories. "He was a lot like my mother. They were very close. She taught him how to ride. They played tennis..." Evelyn's brow furrowed as she gazed out the window. "Sometimes I can still see them sitting together at the piano. Even when he was practically a baby and couldn't really play yet, she loved to hear him bang away and sing. She would laugh so hard..." Evelyn was quiet a long fragile moment.

"Walter, on the other hand, was my father's favorite," she continued in a firmer voice, moving from the window to pace restlessly. "He was named after him, talked like him, even walked like him. But being the firstborn male and all that chauvinistic nonsense..." She waved her hand dismissively. "The point I meant to make was simply that David was an open loving person at one time, and I'd like to think he still is, deep down.

"But when he was sixteen, my mother died. I promised myself when I was walking over here I wouldn't get maudlin about it, and I won't." She lifted her chin and attempted to smile. "Let me just say that she died in a plane crash. My father used to fly his own plane back then, and one Saturday morning they were coming into Newport and the engine failed."

"I'm so sorry, Evelyn."

"Somehow, my father managed to survive, but he was never as vigorous as he'd been before the accident. He died five years later." Evelyn came to sit on the couch beside Diana.

"What a dreadful experience. For you all."

"But for David especially. You see, he'd gone to the airport to meet them. He'd just got his license and was eager to show them how well he could drive."

Diana clutched her hands tightly in her lap. "You mean, he saw the crash?"

Evelyn nodded, and something inside Diana pulled tight, like a fist clenching.

"He was so young and, as I said, very close to my mother. I can't imagine what he went through, being right there, being the one to call the ambulance, and to face the police and all the insanity of the press. But whatever it was, he suffered it silently, all the while taking charge with a strength and self-possession I couldn't pull off even now."

Diana watched a patch of sunlight dance across the floor. Though she still didn't feel any sympathy for the man who'd bullied her at the gate, she felt a kind of heartbreak for the boy in Evelyn's story.

"After the funeral I insisted he come live with me for a while. I'd recently married, and my home was a slightly happier place than Maplecroft in those days."

"Maplecroft?"

"Mm. Our house in Pennsylvania. Walter and Glenda live there now." Diana saw a shadow trouble the woman's expression, and again she wondered about this Walter and why he seemed to disturb everyone so. And Glenda. What part did she play in all this? Her name, so fleetingly mentioned, nonetheless burned in Diana's thoughts as if branded there.

"David stayed with me for two years. It was fun, except...well, I don't know what I expected. Maybe to see him bounce back to the carefree teenager he'd been before the accident. But he'd changed, and there was no going back.

"Oh, everything seemed normal on the surface. He finished school with honors and went on to Harvard. But the David I knew, that open loving boy, had retreated into himself, and he kept on retreating with every..." Her voice trailed off evasively. "Let's just say that David's life hasn't been a smooth one. My mother's death was only the first setback. He's become a cautious, tough and very independent man, Diana, some might even say bitter and disillusioned. But as I said, he wasn't always this way."

Diana sat very still, contemplating Evelyn's words. "I guess this is supposed to have some bearing on my run-in with him, isn't it?"

Evelyn nodded. "Cliff Haven used to be a marvelous place when we were kids. It was David's favorite spot in all the world. And my mother's. But her death changed everything. We came here occasionally after she was gone, but never for long. We sold the horses, all our boats, we cut back the staff. Needless to say, there were no more parties, and we stopped inviting friends. After the accident, the house just sort of went to sleep. Cissy and I started coming back a few summers ago because, frankly, I missed the old place and the happy times. But I guess David's grown accustomed to it lying fallow, so to speak. It's been eighteen years, after all, and any change here upsets him.''

''I see. Especially the kind that comes wielding Mace?''

''That kind especially.'' Evelyn smiled and got to her feet. ''Well, we'd better be getting over to that parade. I guess my story can't make living with David any easier. He is what he is, and I suppose he'll never change. But I was hoping you'd find it in your heart to forgive.''

Diana had the oddest feeling she already had.

CHAPTER FIVE

DIANA'S FIRST TWO WEEKS at Cliff Haven passed pleasantly enough. The only incident that marred the time was Abbie's falling ill. For some reason, the woman went on a house-cleaning binge and then had to be confined to bed for three days. Diana felt terrible. She couldn't help thinking it had come as a direct result of her own cleaning spree at the carriage house.

For the most part, Cissy was a cooperative student. She zipped through grammar and essay lessons with the ease Diana remembered her showing the previous year, and though she didn't like *Moby Dick* very much, at least she was trudging through it with a minimum of complaints.

She was usually happy, too. She spent most of her free time at a nearby yacht club and constantly regaled Diana with stories about her friends there and the comical things they did at sailing lessons.

But she wasn't happy all the time. It was fairly obvious that her relationship with her mother wasn't good, though from scattered comments, Diana surmised that it once had been. Almost every day they went their separate ways, Cissy to the yacht club and Evelyn to visit with friends. When they did find the time to be together, Diana sensed they didn't know what to do with it. Evelyn looked uncomfortable; her conversation sounded stiff and solicitous. Cissy, on the other hand, became critical and sarcastic.

Fridays were the worst, and it didn't take much for Diana to put two and two together and come up with Emmet Thorndike. He usually arrived on Friday to visit for the weekend.

She tried not to think about it, but the situation saddened her nonetheless. She really liked Emmet. She joined him and Evelyn for a round of golf one morning, and it was then that she noticed how easily he could lift the worry lines from Evelyn's face.

Cissy, however, continued to resent him. One evening Evelyn invited Diana to the main house for dinner, and though Emmet tried to joke and cajole away the tension that hung over the table, Cissy's rebellious mood won out.

Later that evening, Evelyn came to the carriage house to apologize. That afternoon she'd told Cissy that Emmet had suggested setting a firm date for a wedding. "I don't know what I'm going to do, Diana. I love both of them so much. But of course, Cissy comes first. If it comes to a choice..." Tears welled up in Evelyn's dark blue eyes. Diana felt so bad for her, for them all, and she wondered if David Prescott had any idea what was happening within his family.

He was gone the entire two weeks, but hardly a day went by that Diana didn't think about him. She thought too about the effect his mother's death had had and often found herself wondering what David felt when he came to Cliff Haven. Did he think about that tragic day when he was sixteen? Is that what he associated Cliff Haven with? Or did he come here to remember how it used to be, those happy summer days before the plane crash? Is that why he'd let the place become frozen in time, like Sleeping Beauty's castle?

She wondered, too, about Evelyn's vague hint of other problems contributing to his remoteness. More than ever she suspected they involved the mysterious Walter, maybe even Walter's wife, Glenda.

But what Diana wondered about most was the Sunday morning David left for the airport. Why had he come up to the carriage house? What would he have said if he hadn't been in such a hurry? And why did he have such a disturbing effect on her? Inexplicable though it was, she'd felt real sparks of attraction flying between them.

In retrospect she supposed it was understandable; he'd looked fairly dynamic that morning, and she had simply responded the way any normal healthy female would. She should be relieved. She was coming back to life after the blow Ron had dealt her.

But...she wasn't relieved. Good Lord, David Prescott? The idea was absurd!

Maybe she'd let down her guard and allowed herself to be attracted to him precisely because he *was* so unapproachable and incapable of responding in kind. Or maybe it was just this place, this fairy-tale setting, which bore so little resemblance to the reality of her life back home.

But no matter what the reason, she knew these stirrings of attraction meant nothing. She still wasn't ready to trust anyone enough to get involved again. Maybe she would change her mind some day, but the man who caused the change would surely be someone a lot more human than David Prescott.

THE WEEKEND finally came around again and with it another invitation to go sailing on Emmet's boat. Diana was glad to learn that Cissy had agreed to join them.

Wearing a long loose blouse over her simple black maillot, Diana met Evelyn and Cissy on the back lawn precisely at noon. They were to meet Emmet down at the pier below the cliff. Diana had been sailing only the one previous time, on the Fourth of July, and frankly she was still nervous.

"Oh, did I mention that David is back?" Evelyn said as the three descended the stairs down the cliff. "Emmet has actually convinced him to come along, too."

Diana's head jerked up and her heart began to race. She glanced out to the small white craft bobbing on the waves, and sure enough, there he was. Who else was so tall, had hair that dark or a back so smoothly muscled?

"And he's got Barbara with him." Cissy sounded as if she were squealing on a naughty brother.

"That's enough, young lady." Evelyn's comment was soft but sharp.

Diana searched the boat. Yes, a third person was indeed with them, a blonde, dressed in a white bikini, sunning herself on the bow.

Diana didn't want to go any farther. David would be angry. This was a private outing. She had no business tagging along. The last person he'd want to see today was *her*, the idiot who'd introduced herself to him with a blast of Mace.

Yet she had no choice but to continue.

David was busy removing sail covers. He was wearing only jeans, tight-fitting faded denims and a pair of scuffed deck shoes. His broad muscled back gleamed like mahogany as he worked. Though he was a tall man, he moved with amazing agility. He turned and his eyes linked with hers. The roar of the ocean died away, and all she heard was the thundering of her heart. She knew what he was thinking: here she was again, the constant intruder!

What *she* was thinking, however, was that she'd never seen such a ruggedly handsome man in all her life. Two weeks had done nothing to put her attraction into perspective. Here under the open sky, he took her breath away.

"Hello, David," his sister said, greeting him warmly. "Welcome back. I hope your trip went well."

He nodded fractionally, his eyes finally leaving Diana's.

"Hello, Emmet." Evelyn climbed down into the boat and shyly kissed his cheek. "Diana, this is Barbara Benedetto, an old friend of ours," she continued, squinting up at Diana, still rooted to the pier. "Barbara, Diana White, a teacher from Fairview who's staying with us this summer."

The look Diana got from Barbara was cool and appraising. "Hello," was all she said. She was attractive and darkly tanned, her long straight hair perfectly streaked by the sun. Diana glanced at David again. She should have known there would be a woman in his life, but why was the reality making her stomach knot up so tight?

Cissy made an ordeal out of getting on the boat, probably because it was Emmet's. First she emptied her duffel bag on the dock, looking for some vague treasure. Then she insisted on brushing her hair.

"Well, are you coming or not?" David finally asked. It was a moment before Diana realized he was looking at her, not his niece.

"Sorry." She took a deep breath and glanced around for something to hang on to. "I—I'm not much of a sailor." It was painfully obvious David didn't want her aboard.

"Here, let me give you a hand," Emmet said graciously, managing not to draw attention to her insecurity. The bow rocked under her feet, causing her stomach to rise and fall.

"Hang in, you'll get used to it," Cissy called, tossing her bag down. Then at David's nod, she unwound a rope from the mooring and leapt aboard like a young gazelle.

Diana found what she thought was an unobtrusive spot, yet she still seemed to be in everyone's way. "Excuse me," they said, stepping over her legs. "Sorry," they murmured climbing over her shoulders. By the time they were out of the slip, she was sorry she'd agreed to come along. She felt like the proverbial fifth wheel, unneeded and unwanted.

Out on the open water, the wind caught the sails and they were off, skimming so fast she lost her breath. Unneeded, unwanted, and now terrified!

"How are you doing?" an exhilarated Cissy called, forgetting she was supposed to be a rebel.

"Okay, I guess." An expert skier, Diana was hardly a stranger to speed and danger. Surely she could adjust herself to this. She glanced up at David and Barbara, so adept at what they were doing. She ached with envy—and admiration. Two more perfect bodies you couldn't find! David glanced back at her as if he'd sensed her attention, and she averted her eyes, feeling painfully self-conscious.

The boat sliced through the water, into the bay, past Jamestown Island and on past Prudence. Diana's blouse was now drenched with spray, and her skin tingled from sun and wind and drying salt.

"Looks like you've found your sea legs," Evelyn called happily from the bench on the opposite site of the cockpit. Diana laughed, realizing she was no longer clinging, white-knuckled, to the gunwale.

They eventually dropped anchor in a quiet cove. Cissy peeled off her T-shirt and immediately dove overboard for a cooling swim while the others lounged in the sun, sipping exotic rum drinks that Emmet had concocted down in the galley.

What David was doing wasn't actually lounging, though, Diana thought. He was sitting slightly apart from the group, as if denying he was part of the social gathering, his whole body alert and restless. He didn't even appear to be listening to the conversation.

But he was. Diana sensed he was taking particular note of the familiarity with which she, Emmet and Evelyn spoke to each other. His jaw became harder with every joke Emmet cracked about Diana's golf game.

Suddenly, doubts about the wisdom of her being aboard returned to torment her. What was she doing here? She didn't belong with these people. Not with *that* person, anyway. Though he hadn't said one word to her since she'd come aboard, she'd been conscious of his attention all afternoon. It was almost a tangible connection, singing like a telegraph line between them. She'd tried to block him out, but it was impossible. She remained as uncomfortably aware of him as he was of her, she was sure.

"Anybody else care to go for a swim?" Barbara yawned and stretched her golden body.

"Looks inviting, doesn't it?" Emmet drawled.

"Sure does." Barbara stepped onto the bobbing bow.

"I've been hoping someone else would want to go in." Evelyn sprang up eagerly. "Diana?"

"Me? Oh, no. I'll pass." Diana was only a fair swimmer, but worse than that, she had no idea how she would get from the boat into the water. Somehow, through all the grueling sessions at the Y and all the summers spent with her brothers down at the pond, no one had ever been able to teach her to dive.

She noticed David get up and gather empty glasses. Then he disappeared below. With him gone, she breathed a little easier. Evelyn and Emmet dove in, sure and graceful, and began to swim toward Cissy who was floating on a rubber raft nearby.

"So, how long are you going to be at Cliff Haven?" Barbara asked. Oddly, she was still standing on the bow.

"Till the end of August." They were the only ones topside now.

"That long, huh? Lucky you."

Diana shrugged. "It's a job."

The blonde smiled coolly. "In case you're wondering, the answer is yes. David and I *are* seeing one another. We have been for three years."

Diana's dark eyes widened. "I wasn't...that's none of my..."

"Sure it is. You've been trying to figure us out all afternoon."

Diana knew she was right. "Whew! Three years! Are you planning to be married soon?"

Barbara choked out a laugh. "Now what would I do with a husband? I've had two of them already. No, no. David and I have something better than a marriage. We have an understanding."

Diana fixed her attention on a distant motorboat, hoping her feelings weren't showing. Not that she understood what those feelings were exactly. They were too numerous and jumbled to sort. The one thing she did know, though, was that they were upsetting.

"It's a wonderful arrangement," Barbara continued. "Whenever either of us needs an escort, we're there for each other. He knows I'm not out for his money, and he's not out for mine. And neither of us is looking for emotional complications. Basically we're both too independent, the no-strings-attached type. Which is probably the reason we've stayed together so long. What about you? Are you interested in David?"

Barbara's forthrightness had Diana spinning. She began to stammer a denial.

"It's okay if you are—honestly. As I said, there are no strings. Only, you'd better be tougher than you look." Barbara's mouth curled in a small pitying smile. "Because David doesn't have romances, honey. He only has affairs."

"I'm really not interested in him in that way." Diana tried to sound sincere, offended even.

The blonde shrugged. "Sorry to have brought it up then. Well, I'm going in. Coming?" Without waiting for an answer, she dove, slicing through the water with hardly a ripple. Diana wished she could do the same, but for heaven's sake, she'd grown up on a dairy farm in landlocked Vermont! Oh well, maybe this time it would turn out all right.

With her heart in her mouth, Diana lurched forward. There was the familiar moment of weightlessness, and then cold water was rushing over her head and up her nose. She panicked and flailed her arms, not knowing which way was up or down. Salt burned her eyes. Her lungs felt crushed. Hell, this wasn't worth it. Pride be damned!

Just then, she felt an arm around her waist—Barbara to the rescue, no doubt. But the arm was too thick and strong, pulling her up to the surface with an ease few women could manage. When Diana shook the water from her eyes, she was startled to find it was David Prescott. Water was streaming down his black hair and glittering on his long spiked lashes.

"Are you all right?" he asked gruffly.

Diana coughed and nodded. He was holding her tightly, crushed against the hard wall of his chest. "I can swim," she said, coughing again.

The corners of his mouth tightened. "Could've fooled me."

Diana pulled back her head as far as his hold would allow and squinted into his eyes. "Where did you come from so fast?"

"I was coming up from below when I saw you hit the water, and since you looked about as graceful as an eggbeater..." He shifted his hold, bringing his right arm more firmly around her waist.

The embarrassing intimacy of being held so close by a man who obviously found her to be the biggest irritant in his life made her indignant. "I told you, I know how to swim."

"Then why the hell did you make me jump in after you with my pants still on?"

"Oh, no! You still have your pants on?"

"Yes, I still have my pants on," he mimicked.

"*Shoot!* I've done it again, haven't I?"

"Done what?"

"Ruined your day."

"Seems so."

"Hey, you two!" Barbara called. "What are you doing, a water ballet?"

Even with ears clogged with water, Diana caught the annoyance in her voice. She flicked a look at David's dark angular face, only inches from hers. Although the water was cool, his muscular chest felt hot beneath her hands. Suddenly it seemed as if she might explode with the emotions churning inside her. She pushed hard and broke away. With short choppy strokes, she struck out for the horizon. She didn't need this; she didn't need to be out on any damn boat; she didn't need a jealous female on her back; and she certainly didn't need a sarcastic malcontent chipping away at her ego and making her feel unwelcome and self-conscious.

When she had nearly exhausted herself—and her anger—she turned and swam back. Streaming water, she mounted the ladder, which, unfortunately, she hadn't seen before her dive. She knew her eyes were blazing with independence. Everyone else was waiting for her. A vague tension filled their silence, as if they'd only that moment stopped talking about her. She chafed her wet arms, feeling a chill that went clear through to her bones. Her heavy tangled hair stuck to her back. Over Cissy's shoulder, she caught the smug smile on Barbara's lips. She obviously found Diana highly amusing.

Well, the hell with Barbara! The hell with all of them! She didn't need any of this.

David had evidently just come aboard, too. He'd thrown a towel over his head and was briskly rubbing the moisture out of his thick hair.

"Let's take her in," he said to Emmet.

Exhausted, wet and cold, Diana slumped to the deck. She drew up her legs and lowered her forehead to her knees. Goose bumps ran up her arms.

As he walked by, David looked down at her, paused and casually dropped his towel. Then he strode off.

Diana picked up the towel—it was quite wet—and glared at his broad tanned back. "How magnanimous!" she drawled. Then, in a rush of anger, she threw it at his head.

Her aim was off, though, and the towel sailed on by and landed in the water. Color immediately flamed across her already sunburned face.

David froze, watching the towel sink out of sight. Then he turned, stiffly.

"I ought to make you go get that," he said, dangerously quiet. Disturbing lights were dancing in his eyes.

Diana had had enough. Her teeth were grinding so hard she feared they'd crack. She noticed another towel slung over a rail not two feet away, and without thinking, yanked it free and sent it flying overboard, too. "Make me! I dare you!"

David's hands bunched into fists, his jaw hardened, and Diana began to think he was going to accept her dare.

But then a strange expression quivered over his lean face, and the hard edges of his features softened. His stern mouth lifted tentatively at one corner, then curved into a smile. The smile broadened, and he threw back his head and laughed. Not a laugh of mockery or derision, it was just . . . a laugh.

Diana stared at him, openmouthed. She didn't know whether he had gone over the edge or what! He had a brilliant smile, a wonderful set of teeth and—yes—even dimples. And his eyes, they crinkled so delightfully.

He suddenly became aware of everyone's fascinated gaze, and as abruptly as the laughter within him had arisen, it ended. He turned and made himself busy, and for the rest of the journey back, Diana was sure she had imagined the whole thing.

CHAPTER SIX

BUT OF COURSE IT HAD happened, and Diana knew her attitude toward David Prescott would never be quite the same. There was a chink in his armor, a soft spot on his heel. He was human after all, perhaps even pleasantly so. She might be dead wrong, but she hoped not, and suddenly she didn't want to give up trying to find out.

They docked the boat at the yacht club, then returned to Cliff Haven in Emmet's car, detouring on the way to drop Barbara off at her condominium.

Once home, Cissy dashed straight into the house in search of a shower, complaining that she was going to be late for a dance back at the club, and Evelyn and Emmet, trying to ignore her continued attempts to rile them, went into the house to see about dinner.

Left alone in the garage with David, Diana's heart pounded unnaturally. He was taking an inordinately long time unloading his belongings from the car, and she wondered if perhaps he hadn't really minded their brush with communication on the boat. Maybe now was the time to share the concerns she had about his family. They'd been troubling her since the day she'd arrived. Maybe this was the moment he'd listen.

"Mr. Prescott?"

"Yes?"

"Would it be too much of an inconvenience if...I mean...could I talk to you for a minute?" Her mouth was so dry her lips were sticking to her teeth.

"What about?"

"Your family."

His eyes narrowed. "What do you mean?"

"Well, there are some problems here you might not be aware of, coming and going the way you do." His scowl became almost too much to bear. "Cissy, for instance. I'd like to talk to you about...her lessons," she finally said, turning coward. She held her breath, expecting him to laugh her right out the door.

"Can it wait till I've cleaned up?"

She gasped audibly in surprise. "Oh, sure. I'd like to shower, too...get all this salt out of my hair."

Still studying her warily, he nodded. "All right. In a couple of hours?"

"I can fix us a light supper if you'd like." The boldness of her offer startled her. Why had she said that? What had possessed her? Now he was really going to laugh.

But he didn't. She couldn't tell what he was thinking. His face was utterly unyielding as he surveyed her, from her sneakers up to her long damp hair. Then he amazed her with a taciturn nod. "Seven-thirty?"

"Seven-thirty."

When she got upstairs, she closed the door and butted her head against it until it hurt. Dear Lord, what had she done? She fell back, disconsolate, onto the couch.

She knew precisely what she'd done. She had just arranged a date for herself with David Prescott!

She sat up and tried to compose herself. So what if she had asked David Prescott over? *He* certainly wouldn't see it as a date. Besides, it wasn't! She really needed to talk to him about Cissy's antagonism toward Emmet and Evelyn's inability to connect with her daughter. She had to let him know about Abbie's fear of growing old and the effect his decision to sell Cliff Haven was having on her. So many problems beleaguered his household—quiet under-the-surface problems that might go undetected if one just flew in for the occasional weekend. David should be told. Maybe he could help.

As Diana glanced at her watch, a whole new anxiety assailed her. It was already six-fifteen, and she didn't even know if she had the ingredients in her kitchen for a peanut-butter sandwich. She jumped off the couch and flew to the refrigerator. All that stared back at her was half a pound of hamburger and a small steak. She pulled open the crisper, yanking so hard it fell right out, spilling its contents. In her frenzy, she left everything on the floor and flung wide a cupboard.

After a thorough search of what was on hand, she decided maybe she would pull this off, after all. She could throw together an Oriental dinner of thinly sliced beef and stir-fried vegetables, served on a bed of rice. She set to work and within twenty minutes had everything sliced, measured and ready for cooking. Then she dashed for the tub.

Miraculously she was ready with ten minutes to spare. Her heart was racing, though, and she wondered how she was ever going to eat. All her former trepidations came flooding back, intensified. What in heaven's name did she think she was doing, inviting David Prescott over for dinner? They had absolutely nothing in common—except their mutual animosity. What would they ever talk about once she'd filled him in on his family's problems, which would take all of about five minutes considering his guarded nature. How would they ever make time pass?

Suddenly there was a firm rap on her door. A wave of nausea washed through her.

"Come on in. Door's open," she called as casually as possible.

Still, when David walked in, she was standing in anything but a casual stance, rooted stiffly by the table, twisting her formal pearls round and round her fingers.

She was surprised to see he was wearing a jacket and tie. He looked casual enough, she supposed. His tan jacket was lightweight cotton and unconstructed, and his pants were brown denim. And yet...

"I brought over some wine. Rosé. Is that all right?"

"Perfect. Thank you."

He walked to the table, looking unfairly tall and assured, and set the bottle down.

"I have some wine open already," she said. "Only half a bottle actually. I'm glad you brought this over. Would you like a glass now?" *She* could surely use one.

"Yes. Thanks."

Diana ducked into the kitchen.

"This place looks different," David called.

She peeked over her shoulder. He was strolling about the living room, picking up framed photos of her family.

"It isn't, honestly." She returned and handed him a glass.

"I wasn't trying to accuse you of anything. Honestly." His gaze met hers, and she realized how automatically she'd become defensive. They each sipped their wine uneasily.

"I hope you don't mind being put to work." The thought of having David Prescott help with the cooking had never crossed Diana's mind before that moment, but suddenly it seemed a wonderful way to defuse the tension between them. "I've got everything ready. It just has to be cooked."

"What are we having?"

"Just a simple stir-fry dinner, I'm afraid. Beef, broccoli, mushrooms, that sort of thing."

"Sounds good. What can I do?" His eyes had a softness to them she'd never noticed before, his eyebrows raised in an arch that gave him an unexpected openness.

"Well, come on into the kitchen. Once the oil is heated, maybe you could stir the vegetables. You can handle that, can't you?"

"If I can't, I'm sure you'll be glad to show me how."

Diana shot him a wary glance, but small mocking lights were dancing in his blue eyes.

"Meanwhile, what are *you* going to do?" he asked.

"Don't worry, I wasn't planning to be idle." As she lit the burners under the fry pan and the rice water, David loosened his tie and undid the top button of his white shirt. "Good idea," she murmured, kicking her high heels off into a corner. "I hope you don't mind refrigerator biscuits. I would've run out for fresh bread if I'd had—"

"Diana, will you please stop apologizing. I'm not fussy."

Diana? He'd called her Diana? She didn't know where to settle her gaze.

"This looks a lot better than my own cooking, and light-years away from the junk I eat on the road."

She glanced up curiously from the sticky biscuit dough. "Do you do a lot of cooking for yourself?"

"Yes, though my talent lies more with Italian dishes."

"Really! Mine ends at tinned spaghetti sauce and a can opener. You can toss in that beef now." She handed him a long wooden spoon, then reached across him to cover the pot of rice. When she did, her arm brushed his shirt front, and the contact, brief as it was, rattled her composure. Good Lord, but this kitchen was tiny!

She sneaked a peek at his face and bit her lip. With his thick dark hair falling attractively over his brow and his skin wind-whipped to a deep healthy bronze, he exuded a masculine appeal she was finding harder and harder to ignore.

"You know," she said, "it's never even occurred to me—I don't know where you live. Where *do* you do all this cooking? You can't be staying in hotels all the time you're away."

"I do much of the time—you'd be amazed. But home, I suppose, is my apartment in New York." His voice was flat and unenthusiastic.

"Why New York?"

He scooped the beef into a bowl and added the broccoli to the pan. "It's home base for all my businesses. The corporate offices are there."

"Really!" She added sliced carrots to the pan and slipped the biscuits into the oven. "For some reason I imagined the steel industry being run from someplace in Pennsylvania."

"Steel?"

Diana glanced at his handsome puzzled face. "A-aren't you the steel Prescotts? Isn't your family—"

"My brother, Walter, controls that end of the business, not me. I'm into other things."

"Oh." Diana stared at the steam rising from the pot of rice for a long quiet time.

Finally he nudged her arm. "Well, aren't you going to ask what kinds of things?" His eyes seemed to bore into her with their bright taunting lights.

She smiled, warming to his unexpected teasing. "What sort of person do you think I am? I don't pry into other people's affairs."

David laughed attractively. "Are you sure you don't want to ask? I'm a fascinating guy. Into everything from racehorses to computer chips."

Diana lowered her eyes. He didn't have to tell her how fascinating he was. Her preoccupation with him these past two weeks had nearly driven her crazy.

"I think everything's ready," she said softly.

At the table David opened the wine he'd brought and re-filled their glasses. Diana lit the candles, and the soft glow wrapped them in a warm intimate circle. He pulled out her chair for her.

"Evelyn lives in New York, too, doesn't she?" Diana asked, trying to hide her reaction to his small kindnesses.

He sat. "Yes, a few blocks from me."

"Oh, how nice. Being close, I mean."

"Except that we don't get to see each other that often. We're all busy." He ladled hot rice onto Diana's plate before serving himself. "But enough about me. Let's talk about you for a while."

She swallowed her wine with a loud gulp. "Me?"

He nodded, smiling a small tilted smile of amusement. "Who are you, Diana White, bane of my life?"

Diana felt prickly heat at the back of her neck. Did David suspect how conscious she was of him? Was he feeling any of that uncomfortable physical awareness himself? Maybe she shouldn't have worn this red dress with the halter top that bared so much of her shoulders. Maybe she shouldn't have left her hair hanging loose.

"I heard you mention a brother once," he prompted.

"I—I don't have a brother, David." She finally found the courage to say his name and almost stopped right there. "I have five."

He put down his fork and stared at her incredulously.

"We grew up on a beautiful dairy farm in central Vermont just a few miles north of Fairview. It's something of a local landmark. You can see the silver silos for miles around. Only Skip and I live there now—everyone else is married. But Dan still comes over to help Skip work the dairy."

David seemed to miss most of this. "Five?" he repeated, stupefied.

She laughed. "Uh-huh. And all older."

He whistled. "Poor kid!"

"Worse than you can imagine. All my life, I've had five extra parents." Her expression became serious. "They're the ones who insisted I bring that Mace to Newport. In case I ran into trouble." David's smile dropped. "I'm really sorry I did that to you, David."

"I survived. But it wasn't a funny stunt to pull."

"I didn't mean it to be. I was terrified." She heard him mumble something. "What did you say?"

"I said I'm sorry, sorry I frightened you." He looked aside, and Diana's heart lurched. It must have taken a great deal for a proud aloof person like David to say those words. She didn't imagine he said them too often.

"Let's . . . let's just put the whole incident behind us, okay?"

She nodded.

"So, tell me more about yourself. This is really delicious, by the way. What ever made you decide to become an English teacher?"

Diana watched the candlelight flickering in his blue eyes. "This is going to sound like a cliché, but it was a teacher I had. In seventh grade." She paused and let her thoughts tumble backward.

"Go on," he coaxed gently.

"I was having trouble in school at the time. Actually, I was failing." Failing, losing weight, getting into school-yard fights. The year she'd lost her mother had been the most painful time in her life, and Mrs. Connelly had realized it and offered to tutor her. Diana knew that had she been kept back, her anger would only have deepened.

But Diana kept the story simple. "She came to my house every afternoon that spring to help me. She was great. She's the one who turned me on to reading. *Anne of Green Ga-*

bles. The Secret Garden. I adored those books. She made me keep a journal, too. I'm still amazed by how much a person can learn about herself by keeping a journal."

David's attention was locked on her face, taking in every shift of expression, every nuance of her voice. "It can be quite cathartic, too," he said.

She shifted uneasily in her seat, suddenly feeling as transparent as glass.

"So, Diana, bane of my life—" his deep smiling voice lifted her out of her uneasiness "—how did you get that bump on your nose?" He poured her more wine.

She touched a hand to it self-consciously. "Is it all that obvious?"

He shook his head. "Quite charming, actually."

She felt herself blush. "Well, it goes this way: once upon a time I got a notion to play Senior League ball."

"Senior League?"

"Yeah, I know. My brothers thought I was crazy, too. Pulling a feminist stunt, they said. But I wasn't. Skip was on the team, George coached, and my other brothers always came to watch. I just wanted to be part of it, that's all."

"You *are* as crazy as I thought. Teenage guys can get pretty rough."

She nodded ruefully. "One day I was waiting in the batting circle and the kid up hitting swung and let go of his bat."

David drew in his breath with a grimace.

"Yep. Wham! Right here."

"Did you continue playing?"

"Not that night." Diana realized she loved hearing him laugh and so provoked it as often as possible. "I did finish the season, though, but most of the time I was scared witless."

"Your brothers must have been glad when you quit."

"Very. They're the kind of guys who used to come home with ruffled organdy dresses for me when I was a kid."

"Your mother died when you were young?" It was more a statement than a question.

"Yes." Diana lowered her eyes. She wanted to tell him she knew he'd lost his mother, too; she knew how hurt he'd been and how deep the scars still ran. But she also knew he never discussed his private life with outsiders.

"I . . . my mother died . . ." he began haltingly.

Diana's eyebrows shot up, and time seemed suspended on that precarious moment.

"My mother died when I was sixteen. In a plane crash. I know how tough it can be." That's all he said, but with that brief admission, Diana felt he'd taken a giant step. Her heart swelled and ached for him. Without thinking, she reached across the table and covered one of his hands with hers.

She realized it was a mistake when David froze. Quickly she drew back her hand.

"Would you care for some coffee, David?"

"Uh...no, thank you." He folded his napkin and placed it alongside his plate.

"So, is there anything else you want to know?" she asked. "Who my favorite authors are? When I lost my baby teeth?"

But David no longer seemed interested. He pushed back his chair and got to his feet. "That was delicious, Diana," he said perfunctorily. Inside her, something budding and vital felt crushed. What had she done? Had that simple touch been all that inappropriate? Did he really dislike her so much that he couldn't wait to get away?

She rose quickly and in her agitation toppled her nearly full glass of wine. Immediately, David snatched up his napkin and started mopping up. She felt her cheeks flaming and tears about to spill over.

"What an oaf! What a clumsy stupid oaf!" she muttered as she dabbed her own napkin over the spreading stain.

"Diana, stop it. Spilled wine is supposed to mean good luck."

"Good luck? Is *that* what you call good luck?" She pointed as the wine dribbled off the table and down his pant leg.

She ran to the kitchen for a towel and knelt to wipe at his shoe. "I'm sorry, David. It seems every time you and I get together, something awful happens, and usually you're the one who gets the worst of it."

"Diana, will you stop it!" He gripped her by the arms and hauled her up from her frenetic mopping. She squirmed unthinkingly, and he held her tighter, closer to him now. Finally she calmed down and dared a look up into his dark enigmatic eyes.

She was amazed by how warm he felt, this man who always appeared so hard and glacierlike. She could feel the heat of his body all down the length of her own. She smelled the clean masculine scent of him, felt the beating of his heart under her sensitive palm, and something coursed through her, a fiery urgency she thought had died forever—only now it seemed brand-new and so much more exciting than she remembered. In the soft candlelight, his thick luxuriant hair glimmered with highlights she longed to touch. His face lost its hardness. His mouth became sensuous and intriguing.

But what frightened her most was the realization that he was looking at her the same way she was looking at him. Something mysterious was passing between them, making them forget who they were, how different their backgrounds, how much they didn't get along. All that mattered was that they were alone together, linked by some powerful wordless bond. Breathlessly, she waited and saw his head lower, and not for a second did she want it any other way.

His lips found hers, brushing them softly at first, tantalizingly. They were warm and tasted of wine. His breath escaped raggedly and became one with hers, and a shudder ran through his body. "Diana," he whispered just before his mouth fell on hers in a deep urgent kiss.

Diana's hands worked their way up his chest and around his broad muscled shoulders, pulling him closer still. His hands moved hungrily over her back, his fingers entwined in her long silken hair. Gently, he pulled back her head and brushed his lips along the smooth pulsing curve of her neck. Then his mouth returned to hers, searing her with a passion she had never known.

When he finally drew away, she was so weak her knees actually buckled and only his arms kept her standing. His heart was beating hard against her cheek. His body, molded to hers, was taut and throbbing.

Her mind was awash, and it was David who finally broke away. He did it so abruptly that she nearly fell over. He turned from her and strode to the door, staring out at the dark night. "I'm sorry, Diana. That wasn't very smart."

As the sensual feelings he'd ignited in her ebbed, an ache gradually took their place. Her throat constricted painfully. Incomprehension filled her eyes.

"Honestly, I didn't plan that," he went on, his voice searching for a cool distant tone. "I make it a rule never to mix my personal life with business. I just lost my head for a minute. I'm sorry."

Oh, was that what she was? Business? One of the hired help? She paused, dumbstruck with the realization that he was right, of course.

"No, David," she said in a proud but breaking voice, "I'm the one who's sorry. Now, you'd better go before I do something really stupid and try to throw you out of your own property."

DIANA AWOKE with a headache. She stumbled to the bathroom, reached for the aspirin, pulled back her tumbled hair and squinted at her reflection. "Diana, you look like hell!" she moaned.

But what did she expect after spending half the night beating her face into the pillow? She hated him. She *hated* him! He had no right to humiliate her—kissing her the way he had and then just dropping her as if he were appalled by the squalid little deed!

It wasn't very smart, he'd said. He'd lost his head. Well, she guessed she had lost her head, too. She swallowed the aspirin with a shudder. She didn't even like David Prescott. He was the coldest, most humorless, unappreciative man she'd ever met. Time and again he'd let her know she wasn't welcome here, not on his property and not in his life. Well, fine! She didn't want him in her life, either.

And yet, there were all those little incongruities that kept pulling her back, whispering in her ear that there was more to him than met the eye. The more she thought about him, the more his cold dictatorial personality fit like a badly cut coat. For a while last night he'd become so easygoing and likable. And when he'd taken her into his arms, she'd wanted to be there more than any other place on earth. Somehow, he, of all people, had turned a key....

She buried her face in her hands and rubbed her swollen eyes. No! The situation had all the potential of a major disaster. She needed to cut him out of her life right now.

He confused her too much. Last night, for instance, she hadn't even broached the subject of his family's problems, and that had been the whole point of his visit, hadn't it? But somehow, caught up in getting to know him, she'd never found the opportunity, and now those problems would only intensify. She should have kept a clearer mind. And he should have remembered to ask. But what really frightened her was the suspicion that neither of them had even tried.

It was a quiet Sunday, muffled by a cool fog. Diana spent two hours of it curled in a chair talking to her brothers. For some reason, their voices sounded rather comforting this gray troubled morning. When she finally got off the phone, she straightened the apartment and gathered a basketful of laundry. Then, dressed in jeans and a red sweatshirt, she hurried across the damp courtyard with her load, taking in deep breaths of the invigorating salt air.

Before she could duck around to the service side of the house, however, the front door opened and she made the mistake of looking back. David was just stepping out. Their eyes linked immediately. He was dressed as he had been the last time he'd left on business, in a suit and tie. From sailing, his skin glowed red-bronze, accentuating the blueness of his eyes.

Diana stumbled to a halt. As if it were happening all over again, she felt the humiliation of being aroused by him and then coldly rejected.

But David was right. Their becoming involved was definitely a mistake. She shifted the weight of the laundry basket, lifted her chin and continued on her way.

"Diana!"

She drew in her breath and slowly turned. He looked tall and calm and utterly aloof. She hoped she looked the same. "What is it?"

A few long strides brought him to her. "I have to leave. I have to go to Michigan for a while."

She was tempted to ask why, but didn't, and just stared at him as dispassionately as possible. "Well, have a good trip."

The corner of his mouth tightened. "Listen, while I'm gone..." He raked back his neatly combed hair from his forehead and paused, thinking. Then, abruptly, he set his briefcase down, took the basket from her arms and set it alongside. "Come on, let's go for a walk." He took Diana by the arm before she had time to protest and propelled her down the path.

"David!" she objected.

"David!" he mimicked with a glint in his blue eyes. She looked at him with a mixture of surprise and alarm. "Come on. It won't take long. I should be out of here already."

On the far side of the house, up a path and half-hidden by vines, stood a small greenhouse. Its glass panes were milky from years of neglect.

"Careful." David held her arm as they stepped over exposed tree roots. He nudged open the reluctant door, then took her hand to lead her through. As he did, a disturbing warmth tingled up her arm and radiated through her body. Her eyes flew to his to see if he felt any of her reaction, but David was a master at concealing whatever was on his mind.

"What *is* this, David?" she asked, forcing her own features into a mask of indifference.

He let go of her hand and slowly surveyed the long wooden benches lined with clay pots. The air was warm and close and smelled of earth.

"Last night I couldn't help noticing how many plants you have. And, well..." He shrugged, looking slightly uneasy, she thought. "We have all these garden tools. If you have any use for them..."

Diana didn't know what to think of David anymore. Just when she decided she had him pegged, he went ahead and surprised her. Her anger began to slip, in spite of her efforts to hang on to it.

She looked up at his sun-bronzed face. They were standing so close she could feel the warmth of his body even through the thickness of his suit. Her breath seemed impossible to catch. Such fathomless eyes! she thought, peering into their blue swirling depths. What was he thinking? Was he remembering last night and the way she'd felt in his arms? Was he thinking of kissing her again?

She couldn't tell, but suddenly she realized she hoped he would. She wanted David to kiss her more than anything else in the world.

But, as if reading her thoughts, he wrenched his eyes from hers. "Diana, about last night..." The tone of his voice sent her emotions plummeting. "It didn't occur to me until later that I probably confused you, maybe even hurt your feelings."

In a flash, Diana realized here was the real purpose for this walk to the greenhouse. And in the same instant she remembered something else, something so obvious she wondered how it could have slipped her mind. "Barbara Benedetto!"

"What?"

"Barbara. Aren't you and she...?"

"Good Lord, no! Barbara and I are just friends."

Diana couldn't look at him. She bent her head and ran shaky fingers along the bench, over a yellowed seed catalog from 1973. "Aren't the two of you... involved?"

"Not romantically."

"I know. I understand." She tried to keep her voice steady. "But you are carrying on an affair."

"Not the last time I looked."

Diana turned to eye him him warily. "Are you sure?"

"Yes, quite. I'll admit we did at one time. Between her marriages. But that was years ago, over and done with."

"And you're not involved with anyone else?" She hoped her lips weren't quivering.

"No!" He thrust his hand impatiently through his hair, mussing it over his forehead.

"Then it's me." As soon as she'd said it, she kicked the ground in disgust. Why had her tone been so peevish? And why did she feel so hurt?

"Diana!" He gripped her arm. "There's nothing wrong with you. Just the opposite. I think you're absolutely..." He let go of her and turned away. He seemed to be silently berating himself. Finally he looked back, once again composed. "I'm just not the kind of guy you'd want to get involved with. I don't have the time or the inclination for romantic involvement. When I do take someone out, it's mostly companionship I'm seeking. That's all. And the women I take out know that clearly."

"And you think I wouldn't understand?"

He studied her features cautiously. "I wasn't sure."

"Thanks, but you don't have to worry. I don't believe much in romance myself."

"No?"

"Trust me, David, if there's anything I don't want in my life right now, it's a relationship."

He expelled a long breath. "Well, that's a relief!"

"That's one of the reasons I was so happy to get a job away from home this summer. My brothers got on a kick of setting me up on blind dates." She lowered her eyes. "We made a mistake last night, but I'm willing to forget it if you are."

"A deal." He held out his hand and she placed hers within it.

She was doing and saying all the things she believed. She was glad they'd had this opportunity to clear the air. And yet why didn't her words ring true, even to herself? Why did she want him to keep holding her hand?

But he didn't. He released it and moved toward the door. They retraced their steps along the path and returned to his abandoned briefcase and her laundry basket, sighing similar deep sighs as they picked them up.

"I have to go."

"Yeah." She looked away. Looking at *him* was too difficult. "Well, have a good week." Or two or three.

He gazed down into her face and for a moment an expression of melancholy seemed to flicker across his handsome guarded features. Gently his hand caressed the side of her face. "You, too." Then he turned and disappeared around the corner of the house.

Diana stared after him for a long time. Her heart was pounding like a frightened animal's. No matter what they had avowed back at the greenhouse, this thing between them wasn't over yet.

CHAPTER SEVEN

Cissy HAD SCOOPED UP her books and was already half out the door when Diana remembered. "Before you go, Cissy, do you realize this Friday is Abbie's birthday?"

"Is it?" The girl paused. "How old will she be, do you know?"

"Seventy-five."

"Wow! I had no idea."

Diana bit her lower lip, hesitating. "I don't know if you people celebrate birthdays in any special way, but I was thinking . . . I would love to throw her a little party. Here, at the carriage house," she emphasized quickly.

Cissy began to nod with growing interest. "Yeah, that would be fun. Turning seventy-five deserves a celebration."

"Of course, I'll clear it with your mother first and assure her it won't be anything extravagant. I'll just bake a cake and invite Abbie over for a visit. It doesn't even have to be a surprise." She didn't expect David to be back. The last time he'd left, he'd stayed away for two whole weeks. Still, she didn't want rumors of a party reaching him. "Does Abbie have any relatives I should invite?"

"Not that I know of."

"Oh, well." Diana shrugged. "I guess it's just us then," she said with a grin. "Oh, I can't wait. Abbie's such a peach."

THE WEEK PASSED in relative calm, except for Wednesday when Emmet came for a visit. He had four tickets to a tennis match at the Newport Casino and insisted that Diana and Cissy accompany him and Evelyn. Diana was thrilled to finally be visiting the Bellevue Avenue landmark. It was the site of the very first tennis court in America.

Cissy, on the other hand, couldn't have cared less.

"But it's the Virginia Slims, Cissy!" Diana coaxed. "Some of the biggest names in tennis are going to be there today!"

"So what! I'm going to miss my sailing lesson." That afternoon, Diana was convinced the girl was an incorrigible brat.

The Casino was lovely with its latticed Victorian porches, flapping canopies and thirteen manicured grass courts. Diana found it easy to imagine she'd traveled back in time to another era, one that was slower, more graceful, and far more peaceful.

The game, however, was anything but slow or peaceful. Diana, who played a little tennis herself, was astounded by the speed and accuracy of a ball hit by a professional. She was enjoying herself so much that she wasn't even aware of the scene developing at her elbow.

She finally did look over, though, as Evelyn's voice rose in frantic whispers. Cissy had removed her shirt, revealing not only a skimpy tank top, but the most hideous tattoos Diana had ever seen. All up her arms and across her shoulders—logos of heavy metal bands, snakes, skulls. Several people were casting discreet, though obviously appalled, glances in her direction. Diana became quite alarmed. She'd passed a tattoo parlor in town...

But on closer inspection she realized the designs weren't permanent.

Smiling smugly, Cissy pulled her shirt back on. Although nothing more was said, the rest of the afternoon was a washout. They didn't go to dinner as planned, and Emmet left for New York right after dropping them off.

THE FOLLOWING FRIDAY afternoon, Diana and Cissy drove to a stationery store in town to pick up balloons and streamers for Abbie's party. Traffic was heavy, it now being late July, and Diana was glad to get back to Cliff Haven.

As her Toyota approached the courtyard, however, every nerve in her body seemed to snap to. David was home. Oddly her first reaction upon seeing him was one of joy, but that passed quickly as all the ramifications of his being back dawned on her.

"Hey, it's Uncle David!" Cissy cried. "I didn't know he was coming home today."

"Neither did I. Oh, Cissy, tonight's Abbie's party, too! What are we going to do?"

"Invite him?"

"Glad to see you think my predicament's so funny."

"What predicament? Why are you so nervous?"

Diana cast her pupil a baleful look. "Cissy, your uncle is hardly a fan of parties, especially parties held at Cliff Haven, and when he finds out I'm the perpetrator, he's going to throw a fit." She peered through the windshield as David crossed the courtyard. Another man, carrying a clipboard and a camera, was with him.

"I don't know how you expect to keep it from him," Cissy said.

Diana sighed disconsolately. "I guess I can't."

"Diana, this is Mr. Sloane, a real-estate appraiser," David explained as she got out of her car. "He's going to take a look at the carriage house. Do you mind?"

Obviously it didn't matter if she did. A week of being away had evidently erased her from his memory. His personality had regained all the crispness of dry toast. Her eyes traveled over his face, searching for a trace of the warmth and humor she'd discovered the previous weekend, but it was gone.

She was furious at herself for being disappointed. What had she expected, anyway? Hadn't they both agreed that their kiss was a mistake? Hadn't they both promised to forget it had ever happened? David was acting the sane one here, and she would be wise to take her cue from him.

"No problem," she answered, tossing her hair with cool indifference. "By the way, I'm having a small get-together tonight for Abbie. It's her birthday." Somehow his coolness gave her the courage—or perhaps the anger—to face him squarely. "You're welcome to come, if you have the time."

He cleared his throat officiously. "Sorry. I'm already locked in to taking Mr. Sloane to dinner. But thanks for asking."

Diana wasn't fooled by his polite phrasing. Ice frosted each and every word.

"You're welcome," she responded in kind. "Follow me, Mr. Sloane."

ABBIE CAME OVER with James at seven forty-five, protesting all the way. "Such a fuss, just because of a silly birthday!" Still, Diana could see she was pleased. The two maids were already there, helping concoct a strong fruity punch.

Diana ladled out five cups and passed them around, keeping one for herself. "Happy Birthday, Abbie," she said, raising her glass. Before she could sip from it, there were more footsteps on the stairs.

"Happy birthday to you, happy birthday to you..." sang a pair of discordant voices. "Happy birthday, dear Abbie. Happy birthday to you." Out on the stair landing, Cissy and a young man took a deep bow. Abbie beamed until her face looked stretched.

They wandered in, and Cissy planted a kiss on the old woman's cheek. "Abbie, this is a friend of mine from the yacht club, Steven Clark." Then she glanced at Diana. "You don't mind, do you?"

"Of course not. Hi, Steven. Come in, make yourself comfortable. But unless you're twenty-one and have a cast-iron stomach, don't try this punch."

A few minutes later, Evelyn and Emmet arrived.

"Miss Evelyn!" Abbie cried in soft astonishment.

Diana carried a tray of drinks across the room. "Thank you for coming, Evelyn. I don't think she expected you. You must know how much it means to her."

"Nonsense. I wouldn't miss this for the world. There hasn't been a party at Cliff Haven in, well, you know. It's wonderful, Diana."

Suddenly the small living room was bursting at the seams with people. Diana smiled. A party! This was turning into an honest-to-goodness party! Well, what was she doing sitting in a corner? she asked herself excitedly. What this room needed was a little music!

They had a perfectly wonderful time. Abbie opened her presents and made a fuss over every one. Then as evening deepened into night, she got to telling stories about the past, stories of rumrunners hiding in the cellar at Cliff Haven during Prohibition, stories about the terrible hurricane of thirty-eight. And when she tired of talking, they put on more music, old brittle records that had been stored there years before—Glen Miller and Bing Crosby, Harry James and several other favorites from the big-band era. Emmet was out of his seat immediately, twirling Evelyn around.

"This is the jitterbug," he announced for the edification of the younger people in the room. "The *real* jitterbug. The one we used to dance to when this music was all the rage."

"Emmet! We're not that old!" Evelyn panted, swinging out limply at the end of his firm grasp.

As Diana slipped quietly into the kitchen to get the cake, she happened to catch a glimpse of Abbie. She was sitting a little apart from the rest of the gathering, a sad smile quivering along her lips. Diana crept back into the room.

"What's the matter, Ab?" she whispered, leaning over.

"Nothing. What could possibly be wrong, child?" But Diana could see moisture glistening on the woman's thin gray lashes. "It's a lovely party. Lovely. Thank you so much. It's just the thing to remember Cliff Haven by when I'm not here anymore."

"Not here? What are you talking about?"

"Well, when David sells this place, what do you think's going to happen? Do you think the new owner is going to want an old hag like me hanging around?"

Diana pressed her lips together tightly as she recalled the appraiser who'd roamed the estate all afternoon. His appearance had undoubtedly made the sale of Cliff Haven a painful reality for Abbie. Unfortunately she could find no words of comfort, only anger toward the man who was at the bottom of this devoted hardworking woman's insecurity.

A peek out the window confirmed that David had returned from his dinner engagement. The sedan was parked beneath the portico.

"Excuse me. I'll be right back," she whispered.

No one except Abbie noticed her slip out the door. She hurried across the courtyard in a defiant long-legged stride, her navy blue dress snapping crisply about her knees. And with every aggressive step she took, she became more convinced that she and the almighty David Prescott were about to lock horns once again!

She gripped the heavy brass knocker and let it fall.

"Yes?"

She jumped. David was the only person who used the intercom. She had forgotten about its existence. "I-it's me, Diana," she stammered. "May I speak with you a moment?"

"I'm pretty busy, Diana."

She summoned her most assertive voice. "I won't be long. It's very important."

Even over the intercom she heard his impatient sigh. "All right. Let yourself in. I'm in the library."

David was sitting in a pool of lamplight, reading at his desk. His white shirt was rumpled and opened at the collar. His dark hair fell untidily over his brow as if he'd passed his fingers through it again and again.

"Don't just stand there," he muttered, flicking a quick glance her way. His gaze ricocheted back almost immediately and swept over her with an attention that made her self-conscious in every fiber of her being. She knew this particular shirtwaist made the most of her tall slender figure. And her hair, which she'd taken time to curl tonight, tumbled in soft waves from two tortoiseshell combs.

"Have a seat," he said, regaining his impassivity almost immediately.

The leather crackled as she lowered herself into it. She folded her hands and watched him sit back, guardedly assaying her. Light from the lamp angled over his face and deepened the stern creases alongside his mouth. Involuntarily she remembered how that mouth had kissed her a week ago, how those eyes had looked down at her, half-closed and drugged with desire.

"Yes?" he prodded. "What did you want to speak to me about?"

"Abbie. Her b-birthday party," she said, her voice wavering.

"Mm. I can hear it clear across the courtyard."

She was about to apologize but then decided not to. The party was on her turf, after all.

"David, what I came over here to say is, Abbie is worried sick about your selling Cliff Haven."

The creases on his brow deepened. "What do you mean?"

"Well, with that realtor showing up, today of all days... She's seventy-five, David. That should explain it all."

"I'm afraid it doesn't."

Diana bit back her irritation. "She's worried that she's too old to be of any use around here."

"That's nonsense. She takes care of the place just fine."

"Yes, she does. But the effort exhausts her. She should have more help."

"Is that what you came over to tell me—to hire more help?" He looked at her with infuriating hauteur, suddenly making her want to shake him senseless.

"Yes. No! I mean, Abbie thinks that if you sell the estate, she's going to be out of a job. She figures the new owner won't want her, and she assumes the old one doesn't, either." She examined the clutter on his desk rather than meet his eyes. "Well, is it true?" she finally asked when the silence grew uncomfortable.

He didn't answer except with a disquieting stare.

"She's been here an awfully long time. Over fifty years. I brought up the subject of retirement once, but she got too agitated to talk. This is the only home she knows. She has no children, no place to go..."

"Well, there isn't much anybody can do about that now, is there?"

Diana stared at him, dumbfounded. "How can you be so dispassionate? After all the years she's worked for your family, there must be something you can do! Surely you can tell her that you'll find her a comfortable place to live. If nothing else, you can put her mind at ease about her financial future."

The room rang with David's silent anger. She knew he wanted her to leave. She'd said enough. She began to get up, then abruptly sat down again.

"I guess that's not really why I came over. For some odd reason, which I will never understand, that old woman loves you. And sometimes," she continued softly, "being loved in return is better than all the monetary assurances in the world."

"So, what do you suggest?" he drawled sardonically. "You seem to have all the answers."

Diana took a deep fortifying breath. "Well, for starters, you could come over to the carriage house. Everyone but you is there."

"Let's just say I don't take too seriously invitations extended at the very last minute."

Diana lowered her eyes. "I'm sorry I didn't invite you sooner, but I didn't think you'd be exactly thrilled about my throwing a party."

He swiveled away from her and walked to the window. Light was spilling from the carriage house. Voices and music rode the breeze. "It's all right. I probably wouldn't have gone, anyway, even if I'd been the first invited."

"Are you sure? I know she'd love to see you."

"Diana!" It was almost a plea. "I have work to do."

She stared at the rigid muscles of his back for a long silent moment. Then, realizing he considered the discussion closed, she rose and went to the door.

A strap seemed to cinch her lungs as she crossed the courtyard. She felt awful—for Abbie, of course, but also for herself, for being so foolish as to think she could get through to that man. At the moment she had serious doubts there was anything to get through to!

Back at the carriage house, the party went on. She lit the candles on the cake and carried it out to the living room, and as she placed it on the table, everyone began to sing.

She was just slicing into it when suddenly something caught her eye—a dark figure out on her stair landing. She flew to the door and opened it wide.

"Come in, David," she said. Her voice had gone breathless.

CHAPTER EIGHT

"UNCLE DAVID! What are you doing here?" Cissy cried.

Diana sensed the others were equally surprised, but mature enough not to express it so vocally. David ignored them and went straight to Abbie.

"Happy birthday," he said, leaning over to kiss her. "How's my favorite girl tonight?"

Diana returned to cutting the cake but cast a glance up to see Abbie's eyes fill with tears. She had a hard time keeping her own from doing the same.

David sat on the arm of Abbie's chair and handed her a present. Carefully she removed the paper and opened the box. Then the tears that had been shining in her eyes finally spilled over.

"What've you got there, Abbie?" Emmet asked.

With badly shaking hands, she lifted out a large silver frame and turned it for everyone to see.

"Why, that's you and Andrew, isn't it?" Evelyn exclaimed.

"Our fifth anniversary, it was." Abbie wiped her cheek and laughed. "Where did you ever get this picture, David? I don't even remember posing for it."

He grinned. "I have my sources."

Diana could see that the framed photograph had been professionally touched up and enlarged from an old snapshot. This was not a gift hastily dug out of a back closet within the past few minutes. Just then his eyes happened to meet hers, and she hoped he saw how sorry she was for her outburst.

Abbie held the frame in both her hands and beamed at it through her tears. "Don't we look grand, though, me and Andrew? I couldn't have weighed more'n a hundred pounds there. And him, with those fancy spats!" She placed it on the coffee table where she could look at it the rest of the night.

The party finally broke up around ten. Diana watched everyone leave from the top of her stairs. David was with them, his arm linked with Abbie's, his head bowed in quiet conversation.

Still stunned, she went back inside and distractedly picked up a few glasses. The living room seemed to echo with conversation and laughter. It had been a wonderful evening, full of surprises.

Suddenly there was a light tap at her door. "Need any help?"

Her heart leapt as she recognized David's deep voice. He strolled in and, without waiting for her okay, began to pick up plates.

She was about to ask what he was doing, but for some inspired reason didn't. This was an overture of some sort. "Sure, I'd love a little help."

In no time at all they had the place straightened. David filled the dishpan in the kitchen and began to wash.

"David?"

He looked up from his scrubbing.

"David," she began again, "I want you to know that what you did tonight was pretty nice."

"No big deal." Then after a short silence, "What you did, having this party, was pretty nice, too."

"You don't mind?"

He shrugged. "Whether I do or not doesn't seem to matter. You go right ahead and do what you want, anyway." Before she could decide if he was reprimanding her, he reached out and dabbed a mound of soapy foam on her nose. He smiled, and the smile transformed his whole face. "I'm not trying to make excuses for myself but, well, I have thought about Abbie. I've thought about bringing new people in to help, but I've always been afraid she might think I was trying to replace her. Same reason I never asked her to retire."

"Oh, David. I'm sorry."

"Don't apologize. I didn't realize she was so worried until you told me."

"And now that you do?"

"I offered her the position of head housekeeper at my apartment in New York. I know she'd prefer to live out the rest of her life here, but it's the best I can do. And she seemed happy enough with the arrangement."

How easily David had found a solution! A very personal solution, too. And all it had taken was a little nudge. In her elation Diana wrapped an arm around his neck and gave him a tight spontaneous hug. He looked uneasy and set to scrubbing a glass with unnecessary vigor. Still, he wasn't stiffening the way he had last weekend when she'd reached across the dinner table to touch his hand.

Before long the dishes were done and they were walking into the living room. "Thank you, David. I really appreciate your help. Would you care for a cup of coffee?"

He paused at the screen door. "No, thanks. I've got to get back to my work." He rested a hand on the door latch and sighed with reluctance.

"Nice night, isn't it?" Diana peered into the hot humid darkness. Crickets were chirruping in the shadows below the stairs. The surf was a low distant roar.

"Well..." David stepped onto the landing and glanced up at the full yellow moon.

"Good night, David, and thanks again."

Suddenly he was back in the room. "Diana, are you very tired?"

"Not really." Her pulse began to race.

"Great! Let's go for a sail."

"W-what?"

"I've had too much coffee, I'm restless as hell, and the last thing I want to do is go back to those damn books. Let's go for a sail."

"Where? How?"

"In my new boat." He laughed with boyish glee. "I didn't realize how much I missed sailing until I went out on Emmet's."

"So...you bought a boat?"

He nodded. "It was an impetuous thing to do, I know, but I didn't go out and get anything big or elaborate."

"But...I don't feel like going sailing. I don't even like sailing."

"That's just because you don't know how. Go on, go change into something more comfortable."

Openmouthed, Diana stared back at him over her shoulder as she hurried to her room. Telling herself that she'd lost her mind, she slipped out of her dress and into jeans and a T-shirt.

"But it's nighttime," she protested, even as David propelled her down the stairs. "Isn't it dangerous to go sailing at night?"

He arched his eyebrows in a comic leer. "Extremely." Inside the garage, he walked right by the sedan and headed for his motorcycle.

Diana's feet riveted to the cement floor. "Do we have to go on that thing?"

He nodded.

"But why?"

"But why?" he mimicked.

"Don't make fun of me!"

"Wouldn't dream of it. Here." He lowered a helmet over her head and gently tucked her hair inside.

"I'm not getting on that thing!"

"Okay. You can run alongside." With that, he swung his leg over the bike and started it up.

By the time they reached the yacht club, Diana was thoroughly shaken. "You drive like a maniac!" she hollered.

"I beg your pardon!" he said, feigning mild affrontery. In his eyes small flames danced like devils.

"You must have been doing seventy around some of those curves!" She pulled off her helmet and flung it at him.

"Admit it, you loved it." He turned and strode down the dock without waiting for her. With disconcerting agility, he leapt onto his sleek new boat and held out a hand. Diana's stomach turned over.

"No, David. Forget it."

He retracted his hand and dragged it through his hair. "What is it now?"

"Sailing at night is dangerous, isn't it? I want you to really level with me."

He shook his head. "The water's calm as glass, the wind's only about three knots, and I could navigate these waters with my eyes closed. If that's not enough, there are six life jackets on board, and you can wear them all, okay?" He held out his hand again and his dark brilliant gaze locked with hers. "Trust me," he said in a low whispery voice.

Though her knees were knocking, Diana let him take her aboard. He started the engine, and slowly the graceful white hull backed away from its mooring and headed toward the open bay.

"Di, come here a minute," he called. "I want to teach you how to hoist a sail."

Di? Her heart leaped inexplicably. Her brothers sometimes called her Di. Close friends did, too. Had David unwittingly crossed a threshold into their ranks? Was he feeling so comfortable with her that the nickname had just slipped out?

They sailed a slow arc around the island, following the mansion-studded coast. When they passed Cliff Haven, David pointed it out to make sure she didn't miss it. Moonlight glazed the entire estate. More than ever, it looked like Sleeping Beauty's castle.

"It's awfully impressive, isn't it?" she said softly, surprised by the depth of fondness she felt for the place. She looked into David's face. He was sitting close enough to reach over if necessary and adjust the rope she was holding. His closeness was reassuring. "David, why do you want to sell Cliff Haven? It's so beautiful, and it's been in your family since it was built."

She could almost feel the tension rise like a tide up his body.

"Sorry. I guess it's none of my business." She lowered her eyes, hoping she hadn't spoiled the good mood that had opened up between them tonight. Besides, she already suspected the reason. The bad memories he associated with Cliff Haven apparently outweighed the good. Selling the place would be an emotional unburdening.

"Okay," he finally conceded. "I'm selling Cliff Haven because . . . because it's not cost-efficient."

Diana's breath exploded in an abrupt little laugh. "It's what?"

"I'm serious. It's far too expensive for what I get out of it. I rarely use it during the winter, yet it has to be heated. Taxes are atrocious. There's a never-ending upkeep bill, and even during the summer I'm too busy to spend any significant time here.''

"Oh, so it's just a matter of balance."

"Of what?"

"Balance. In other words, if you got more out of the place, then it would be worth the expense?''

"Don't put words into my mouth. I never said that." He reached around her and adjusted the rope she held. For a moment, the brush of his body against hers made the simple act of speaking impossible.

"B-but it's true, isn't it?" she resumed with difficulty. "If you stayed longer, went sailing and played tennis, entertained clients here, got a few horses . . ."

"Hey! Slow down!"

She tensed again. "Sorry. I run off at the mouth sometimes. I realize I have no right arguing the pros and cons of selling Cliff Haven with you. It's your house, your life . . ."

"Exactly."

It was a crisp reply, and she knew she was pressing her luck by adding, "Forgive me?"

"No!"

"It's going to be a pretty long night unless you do."

David threw up his hands. "All right! Forgiven. Just as long as you shut up!" And then he erupted in an involuntary laugh. Diana laughed, too. She liked this bantering far more than the aloofness he'd tried to affect earlier in the evening.

With her tentative help, David headed up into the Sakonnet River along Acquidneck's east coast. She felt heady with a sense of accomplishment. Soon the river narrowed. Farmlands and pastures rose up from grassy marshes to meet moon-washed barns and old New England homes.

"It's so peaceful here," she commented. David, who was busily taking down the sails, smiled, and it seemed to her that a quiet pride entered his eyes. He'd probably sailed these waters innumerable times, as a boy growing up, as a daring teenager.

"Di, lower the anchor for me, will you?"

Di again. The name sounded so personal, so intimate, coming from him. She blinked. "The anchor? Why?"

"Because if you don't, the boat will drift off while we're swimming."

"Who said anything about swimming?"

"I did. You don't happen to be wearing a bathing suit under those clothes?" he asked, giving her jeans and T-shirt a quick but decidedly approving glance.

"No. But that's perfectly all right. I don't feel like swimming, anyway," she said, watching the dark current slide by the boat.

"Of course you do. On a night like this, the river's probably like bath water. As still as a Vermont cow pond, too."

"Cute." She tried to look vexed, but he was slipping off his pants, and her eyes couldn't help skimming over the corded muscles of his long legs.

"Di, don't get all excited now, but I didn't bring a suit, either."

"You...you're not!"

Off came the shirt, and suddenly David was standing there just in his underwear. His chest was broad, his stomach hard and flat. For a moment the air seemed insufficiently thin as she tried to catch her breath.

She chided herself for reacting to him this way. All night she had kept a firm rein on her emotions, knowing there was nothing she needed less in her life than a man—especially this man! But for a moment, watching him remove his clothes, reason had abandoned her.

"Don't go any further." She pointed an unsteady finger at him.

"Wasn't planning to—though it's a perfect night for skinny-dipping. Now, what are we going to do about you?"

"Nothing. I'm staying right here, thank you."

"I wouldn't suggest going in wearing those jeans. They'd get too heavy."

She was about to protest again, but he'd already stepped to the edge of the bow. Then in perfect form, his magnificent body arced forward and sliced through the dark surface.

Diana peered over the side with growing anxiety. Eventually he emerged, yards away, his dark hair sleeked back from his high forehead, his strong muscled shoulders gleaming like polished mahogany. For a moment, her heart stopped. A sea god—that's what he reminded her of. Neptune rising from the ocean depths. She could feel a small bemused smile chasing her vexation.

"I can't describe it, it's that good," he called out. "Come on, jump in or I'll throw you in myself."

"No! I'll go in on my own!" She kicked aside her sneakers and pulled off her jeans—but she would keep on her long T-shirt no matter what he said. She inched to the edge of the prow and raised her arms over her head.

But when she peeked down at the water, panic took hold of her. "I can't."

David swam toward the boat. "You can't? What are you talking about? You're a good swimmer."

"It isn't that." She hesitated. "I ... I can't dive."

David was silent one brittle moment, then he began to laugh. She regretted the day he'd first laughed at her because, having started, he seemed to indulge in it every chance he got.

"It's not funny!"

"Can you jump in?"

"That's a little easier, though I still get that feeling in the pit of my stomach. You know, like riding down sixty stories in an express elevator. Once I'm under, I begin to think I'm never going to find the surface. And at night..." She shivered.

David blinked up at her. His lashes were incredibly long and silvered with water and moonlight. Did he understand? If only he could see her ski, she thought. She'd learned at four. Took the women's downhill two years in a row at college.

But as soon as the thought struck her, she wondered why it had. What was this urgent need to shine in his eyes?

"I'll be right here," he reassured her. "If you can't find the surface, I'll haul you up by your hair. How's that?"

Diana rolled her eyes. "Terrific!"

"Trust me," he said, smiling rakishly. "I'll be right here."

Her toes curled over the side. Then, with a sudden surge of adrenaline, she dove into the water. She emerged, spluttering, about two feet from David. Her thighs were stinging.

"How'd I do?"

"I'd forget the Olympics if I were you. But for one July midnight on the Sakonnet River, it wasn't too bad."

Just as he'd promised, the water felt wonderful, like warm silk against her skin. It didn't take much to persuade her to swim to a tiny island nearby. It was only about thirty yards, he said, and the current was with them.

When they finally reached the island, though, she felt a rush of relief. She staggered forward, muscles quivering, and collapsed onto a patch of thin grass. Her shirt clung uncomfortably, and the night air, humid as it was, felt cold on her skin.

David sank down beside her and was quiet while she caught her breath. Lying on his back, he stared up at the hazy moon through the thin leaves of a sapling. A breeze rustled over the water and raised a chill on Diana's body.

"Cold?" he asked softly. She nodded. He lifted himself up on one elbow and rubbed her wet arms, trying to warm her. It was an innocent-enough gesture, she supposed, but it made her much too conscious of herself as a woman and of him as an extremely desirable man.

She sat up. "We should be getting back," she said nervously. Swimming out to this island with him had been foolhardy.

"Let's wait. The tide will be changing soon and the current will be in our favor again."

"How long?"

"An hour. Maybe a bit more."

"You don't know, do you? For all you care, we could be stranded here forever."

His mouth curved into a soft amused smiled. "Don't you ever shut up?" he said lazily. "Here we are alone on an island, the moon couldn't be bigger if it tried, and all you can think about is what time the tide is changing." He shook his head disparagingly.

Diana swallowed hard, staring into his heavy-lidded languorous eyes. And what might he be thinking about? she wondered.

As if reading her thoughts, David reached up and caught a handful of her long wet hair and slowly pulled her down to the grass beside him. All the air seemed to be sucked out of the night. She couldn't breathe, or speak, or think. All she knew was that his arms were wrapping around her, gathering her close. Their bodies pressed together, and then he was kissing her, exquisitely, passionately, the way no man had ever kissed her before.

Reluctantly he raised his head and looked into her eyes. She smiled. It felt so right, so natural to be in his arms. Ever since the previous weekend when he'd kissed her, she'd been able to think of little else. They may have claimed it was a mistake, but she'd known even then that theirs was an attraction too strong to forget. Not even David, who commanded an iron will over his emotions, could ignore the chemistry that flared between them. It frightened her. It was blind unreasoning attraction. But it was also thrilling. She felt heady and alive in a way she never had before.

She reached up and buried her fingers in his hair, pulling his head down. Her lips parted and his mouth touched hers once more in a deep probing assault that toppled the last of her reservations and turned her bones to water.

She could feel his body becoming insistent. He moved over her, his weight pressing her to the ground. His long legs entwined with hers.

"Diana," he said, his sensuous whisper sending small waves of heat licking through her body. She gazed lovingly at the black hair framing his leathery face, ran a finger down his beard-coarsened cheek to the mouth that now looked so sensitive and passionate. He kissed her fingertips.

"David, I don't understand this." Her voice was a helpless whisper.

"I know. When I went away last weekend, I was so sure I could ignore you the rest of the summer, but you have an insidious way of getting under my skin."

"Thanks. You make me sound like a disease."

"You are. A very dangerous one, too." His eyes smoldered as they traveled across her face. His hand ran lightly over her wet hair, smoothing it. "Why you?" he whispered almost to himself. "What's so special about *you* that made me come running back home two weeks before I intended to, hm? I don't even like you." His mouth curved in a sensuous half-smile. "You're a smart-mouthed nuisance who insinuates her way into everybody's business, invited or not. You talk too much, and you can't dive worth a damn.''

Diana curled closer into his embrace, drugged by his low soft voice. ''Maybe it's not to understand,'' she answered. ''Maybe we shouldn't even try.''

David's face went deadly serious. Then he pulled her into the warmth of his body and kissed her until neither of them was capable of logical thought.

After a few minutes, nothing mattered. Nothing and no one existed beyond the small private world that enveloped them. Their bodies lifted toward each other, tightening into knots that strained to be released.

David's hands roamed over her freely, spreading waves of heat wherever they went. When he worked his way under her shirt and found the firm swell of her breasts, the heat between them leapt into flame.

Suddenly voices were whispering in her ear, voices she didn't want to hear. David was a man who never got involved. He didn't have the time for love. He only had affairs. But even if his intentions *were* noble, she had nothing in common with him. They came from different worlds. When her work was done at Cliff Haven, their paths would never cross again. And if she got too close, if she opened her heart too wide, she was bound to get burned.

''David, please, let's stop,'' she murmured against his lips.

''Di, I want you. More than I've wanted anything for a long time. Please...'' His hand moved slowly from her breast down to her waist and over the smooth length of her thigh. A wave of debilitating heat washed through her. Still, she managed to sit up.

''No! This is crazy!'' she said as firmly as she could.

He rolled away from her and lay still for a few seconds. ''Why not?'' His voice was tight with frustration.

"Because I don't want to."

"Don't lie." He shielded his eyes with his arm as if he didn't want her to see whatever lay within them. The gesture tugged at her heartstrings.

She stroked his hair lightly, only to have him shake her off with a hurt angry snap of his head. She curled up her legs and wrapped her arms around them. "David, you don't understand." Her voice was husky with impending tears. "I do want to make love. I'm very attracted to you." She was appalled by the easy way she was admitting to him what she'd been unable to admit to herself. "But we hardly know each other, and when the summer's over, we'll never see each other again. It would just be an impetuous physical affair, a one-night stand, simply because we happen to be alone under a full moon. And I can't live with that. When I make love, I expect love and commitment to be involved, too." She paused. "Are you listening to me?"

He sat up and gazed at the water gently lapping at their feet. "Commitment," he repeated sardonically. "And by that I suppose you mean a marriage license."

"Yes. Or the prospect of one in the near future."

He picked up a pebble and flung it into the water. "I told you last week how I feel about all that. I don't have time for emotional complications, Diana." He reached over and stroked her back. "What a pity," he murmured. "We're so naturally attracted to each other, too. I bet we'd light up the sky with our lovemaking."

He lifted aside her hair and ran his warm lips over her shoulder. Diana trembled with reaction. Then he turned her to face him and kissed her so persuasively that she almost changed her mind. But she knew she'd be sorry if she did.

Powered by a strong sense of self-preservation, she pulled away and stared levelly into his half-closed eyes. "No,

David!'' Her hands on his bare chest rose and fell with his heavy breathing.

"You know it wouldn't be hard for me to take you by force."

"I know. You're a lot bigger and stronger than I am. But even though I haven't known you long, I know you'd never do a thing like that."

He swallowed with difficulty. "How can you be so sure?"

"You don't play the tyrant very well." She smiled, letting her head fall so that his lips were on her forehead. "David, all night you've asked me to trust you, and I have. I was afraid to come sailing tonight. I was afraid to dive off the boat, afraid to swim to this island. But I did. I did it all, not to provoke you, but simply because...because you asked." She finished softly, her voice trembling with sincerity. "Now I'm asking something of you." She raised her head so that their eyes met. "Don't press me into making love. I'm not ready."

His dark eyebrows nearly met in puzzlement.

"You see, last year just about this time, I was supposed to be married, but a week before the wedding, my fiancé called it off. To make a long story short, I got burned. To a crisp. I lost a whole lot when we split up—my pride, my self-esteem and confidence, and I've been unable to get involved since. I guess I'm scared of being hurt again. So I have to be very careful. And I have been. I haven't become involved with anybody so far. Though, to be perfectly honest, nobody has come along who's interested me. Until now." She paused, wondering what it was about this man that prompted her to bare her soul. He himself was the most uncommunicative person she'd ever met. "David, I feel very close to you right now. Already I feel more for you than..." She paused. No, she couldn't possibly mean to say Ron, though that was the name on her lips. "But I can't make love with you. For one thing, it's not in my nature to have a casual summer affair. But more importantly, even it it were, I'm not ready. I'm scared . . .''

At that moment, there wasn't a single barrier between her and David. He was listening to every word she said, his eyes so clear she was sure she could see right through to his soul. And what she saw was an understanding and compassion so deep it momentarily startled her.

He tucked her close and rested his cheek on the soft crown of her hair. And there she sat, wrapped in the protective warmth of his arms, until she began to think he would never let her go.

CHAPTER NINE

"THERE'S A POT in here, but I can't find the coffee," Diana called from the galley.

"Are you decent?"

"Always." When David looked in, she twirled around. His warm fisherman's knit sweater swung about her knees.

"Lovely." He winked and ducked into the cramped quarters. "It's in the cupboard over the sink. Here, let me get it."

A few minutes later, they were sitting across from each other at the small table with steaming mugs in their hands.

"So, this creep...Ron? How do you feel about him now?"

"Still a bit angry."

"That all?"

She thought awhile. "Uh-huh. Funny, isn't it? Last year my world revolved around him and now—" she shrugged "—nothing."

"It happens."

Diana glanced at David curiously. "To you? Have you ever been jilted by someone you really cared about?"

"Of course not. Not me." He reached across the table for her hand and touched it to his lips.

Diana felt light-headed with the easy intimacy that flowed between them. It seemed like they'd been friends forever.

"I've been dying to ask you something, David. How did you get that little scar on your lip?"

He laughed quietly, squeezing her hand. "You're probably hoping I'll reveal a dramatic tale about a fencing duel or something, but it's nothing like that. I just fell down a flight of stairs when I was two."

"Eow!"

"But if you want me to embellish it, I could tell you my brother probably pushed me."

Diana's attention sharpened.

"It was all Evelyn's fault, though. She used to pay too much attention to me, constantly dressing me and brushing my hair as if I were one of her dolls. I think Walter was secretly jealous." Although the story was supposed to be amusing, David's smile faded. He retracted his hand and stared at his coffee mug.

"You and Evelyn have a special relationship, don't you?"

He looked up, his eyes still slightly unfocused. "Why do you say that?"

Diana's heart beat with anxiety. Yet she felt they'd grown closer tonight, and she could say almost anything to him. "She...she told me what you went through when your mother died."

David's shoulders tightened perceptibly. "Oh."

"She mentioned that you went to live with her, too."

"Yes. I'll never forget her kindness."

"David? Can I ask you something else? What kind of relationship do you have with your brother?"

David sipped his coffee meditatively. It was none of her business and he was probably thinking as much. But then he shrugged. "What can I say? When I was growing up, I idolized him. He was my big brother."

"But you don't see each other anymore..."

"Damn right we don't." Bitterness hardened his mouth.

"Well, that's what I'm asking, I guess. What happened between you two?"

"You don't know?"

"No."

"Honestly?"

"No!"

He subsided with a sigh of resignation. "After my father died, Walter and I came to blows over settling the estate."

"Wasn't there a will?"

"Yes, but my father wasn't himself toward the end, and to this day I believe Walter had too much of a hand in drawing up that will. I was in college at the time, so I was unaware of what was actually happening, whereas Walter was in the perfect position to exert his influence. The will gave him full authority over the disposition of the estate. And while I didn't mind Walter naming himself chairman of the holding company, I can't imagine that my father really wanted him to have seventy percent of the stock." David's eyes still looked painfully angry, and Diana could only wonder what he'd felt at the time of the argument.

"Of course," he went on, "Walter graciously conceded ten percent to me and Evelyn, with the remaining stock being in the hands of shareholders. Evelyn got an additional cash settlement, and I got the rest of my father's interests. But they were just a handful of tired old factories that Walter had no interest in and were about to fold anyway."

"And Cliff Haven?"

"And Cliff Haven, which is a barn compared to our house in Pennsylvania."

"Which Walter kept for himself."

"Right. That really knocked the wind out of me, being railroaded by my own brother. It certainly opened my eyes. No matter what you've been told, Diana, the meek do not inherit the earth."

"So, what happened after that? What did you do after you found out you'd been cheated?"

A muscle along his jaw twitched. "In spite of a lengthy court battle, there wasn't much I could do. I finished school and then went to work on those wrecks Walter generously let me have." In the silence that followed, he slowly began to smile. "Funny things, those wrecks..."

Diana didn't like the way he was smiling. It was an expression she imagined *Moby Dick*'s Ahab capable of. "They're the ones you still own today, aren't they?"

He nodded with immense satisfaction. "And Walter's blue-chip stocks have been dropping ever since!"

Diana didn't like the sound of his laugh, either. David had undoubtedly been deeply hurt and as a result had turned bitter and perhaps vengeful.

"So you haven't spoken since?"

David was quiet a long time, his eyes fixed on the table-top. Watching him, Diana got the strangest feeling there was something else lying back there in the past, something he was thinking about right now. But as close as they'd become, he wasn't about to tell her.

"No, we haven't spoken," he finally said.

"Don't you ever miss him? I mean, gosh, he has a wife, two boys who are your nephews..."

A curious shadow passed over his features and he blinked a few times. But then he lifted his chin with unyielding pride. "No. They mean nothing to me." And the subject was dropped.

THANK HEAVEN it was Sunday! Without even bothering to remove David's sweater, Diana fell into bed and went to sleep. When she awoke, her clock confirmed that it was just before noon. With a small contented smile, she wrapped the thick sweater closer and breathed deeply of a fragrance that was distinctly David's. Then she arose, feeling remarkably refreshed, and took a long hot shower.

She was combing the last tangles out of her hair when there was a knock at her door. It was David, leaning cavalierly against the door frame. "Hi." He smiled through the screen.

"Hi, yourself." She was amazed at how happy she was to see him again. "What are you doing up so early?"

"Diana, it's almost one o'clock!"

"Sure. But when you go to bed at five a.m., one is early."

"May I come in, or do you have a thing about talking through screens?"

Diana giggled and opened the door. Much to her surprise, he brushed a light kiss across her lips. Because it seemed so unthinking, she found it utterly endearing.

"I don't suppose you've had breakfast yet?"

"Uh-uh. What's that you're carrying?"

"Croissants. If you'll put on some coffee, I might even let you have one."

"You've got yourself a deal, mister." Diana fairly danced into the kitchen.

They decided to make a picnic of it, changing into swimsuits and taking the croissants and coffee down the cliff to a small sandy cove. Sitting cross-legged on her blanket, feeling the hot sun on her back, Diana nearly purred with contentment.

"I feel positively hedonistic," she confessed, wiping the last crumbs off her thighs.

David watched her with a small pleased smile. "You do have a knack for making feasts out of simple pleasures."

"They're the best kind."

The dark hair on his chest glistened in the sun. She studied the way it ran down to his hard flat stomach and disappeared in a vee at the waistband of his trunks. He had an incredible body. It was no wonder she had reacted with such volatility to him last night out on the river.

She tried to clear her mind of that disturbing memory by reaching for the book in her canvas bag.

"What are you reading?"

"Stendhal. *The Red and the Black.*"

"Oh, nothing to do with Cissy's work, then?"

"No. Just for my own pleasure."

"Have you reached the part where Julien has been caught with the mayor's wife and is running across the yard with the watchdogs at his heels?"

Diana shook her head.

"It's priceless. I've always thought it would make a hilarious scene in a movie." He paused, his eyes growing wary. "What's the matter?"

"You! When did you ever read Stendhal?"

"What? Don't you think I know how to read?"

"Well, when I was in school, I wasn't always that sure about you people in business."

"What a snob!"

"I am not!"

"You are. But that's beside the point. Where'd you get the idea I took a business degree?"

"Well, I . . . what *did* you study?"

"You ask too many questions." He sat up and removed a hairbrush from her bag. "Turn around." He positioned her between his legs and began to brush her hair. Diana closed her eyes and succumbed to the relaxing sensation washing over her.

"You have terrific hair, y'know that?"

Diana wasn't sure if her goose bumps rose from the gentle stroking or from the compliment. With surprising adeptness, he braided her hair and secured it with an elastic. When he finished, he planted a light kiss on each of her bared shoulders, then turned her around in his arms. The closeness of his lips made her mind reel.

"Archaeology," he whispered.

Diana blinked through her languor. "What?"

"Archaeology. That's what I studied."

"You're kidding!"

"Uh-uh. I was going to travel the world uncovering lost civilizations."

"Really?" She lifted her fingers to his forehead, brushing aside the breeze-tossed hair. "It doesn't seem fair, your life being rerouted just because of Walter's greed."

He leaned into her soft caress. "I made my own choices. I don't blame him for *that*."

"Do you miss it, the archaeology?"

"No. It was a fascination of my youth. Like love." He closed his eyes as she traced a pattern around his lips. Finally he grabbed her wrists. "Diana, for heaven's sake. I'm only human. Stop teasing."

Her cheeks warmed. "I . . . wasn't aware . . ." She moved away and wrapped her arms around her knees. "So, back to archaeology. Are you sure it was just a fascination? I hate to see people trapped in occupations they don't like."

"I do, too. That's why I'm in business. I may have fallen into it by default, but I've stayed in because I discovered I love it."

"I don't know, David—all that corporate raiding that's going on today, junk bonds and mergers . . ."

"I agree. It's pretty empty. That's why I'm not into any of that."

"Then, what . . . ?"

He laughed in exasperation at her persistent questioning. "Manufacturing, pure and simple. I love producing things. Come on. Let's go for a swim."

The surf was strong, and David taught her how to catch the waves just as they were peaking and ride them all the way to shore. In the water, he became uninhibited and boyish, whooping with joyous expectancy as each new wave was about to curl over him. Diana had never imagined he could have so much fun.

Finally they dragged themselves up from the surf and collapsed on the blanket, exhausted and tingling all over. She turned to look at him. His eyes were closed, his dark hair sleeked back. Water was drying on his cheek.

"By the way, how's Cissy doing these days?" he asked, interrupting her quiet admiration.

"Fine, as far as her schoolwork is concerned." She sat up and sifted sand through her fingers. "David?"

"Mm." His voice was deep, sleepy, sexy.

"Have you noticed the tension between Evelyn and Cissy lately?"

He opened one eye and frowned. "Is there tension?"

"Uh-huh. And I think that's why Cissy failed English this year."

He sighed resignedly and sat up. "Am I about to hear another one of your theories about my household, Miss White?"

"But I was right about Abbie, wasn't I? *Wasn't* I?"

He nodded grudgingly. "So, what do you think Cissy's problem is?"

"Well, it all stems from the fact that Evelyn and Emmet want to get married, and Cissy feels that she's—"

David's hand suddenly clamped over her arm. "Get married? Evelyn and...? Whoa! Back up, Diana."

She stared at him incredulously. "Didn't you know?"

"Would I be making such an ass of myself if I did?" He loosened his hold and turned his dazed blue eyes on the horizon. "Married. Well, I'll be damned!" But almost immediately he swung back to her. "How is it that *you* know what's going on and I don't?"

"Because you're always too busy to open your damn eyes!" The vehemence of her answer dismayed her. He'd take offense.

"I know I'm busy, but I never figured..." He paused, lost in thought. "You say Cissy's not too crazy about this upcoming marriage?"

"Right. Of course, she won't always admit it in so many words..."

"It just sneaks out in failing grades."

"Right again. She's had her mother's undivided attention for so long, I guess she feels threatened now. She has to win back that attention any way she can, even if the means are self-destructive." She paused and lowered her eyes. "That's my opinion, anyway."

"Sounds plausible. The outrageous makeup, the pouting..."

"It's usually when Emmet's around, too. She loves to do things that cause him misgivings about becoming her stepfather."

David's lips tightened. "You know, I think you're right."

"I think so, too," she said. "But the biggest danger I see in this war she's waging is that she and her mother might drift so far apart they won't know how to get back together again."

David rubbed the side of his face. "Do you have any suggestions?"

She didn't like the flinty look in his eye. "I wouldn't feel right suggesting anything. It isn't my place."

"But if it were?"

"Well—" she sighed "—Evelyn and Cissy should spend more time together, and maybe the summer isn't enough. As

I see it, the problem might be eased if... if Cissy didn't go to boarding school."

"Prescott kids have always gone to boarding school."

"So? Maybe it's time to break with tradition. If she were living at home, at least she'd be part of her mother's new life instead of feeling shut out." Diana felt uneasy. David was looking at her with the same angry expression he'd worn the first time they'd met. "I'm sorry. Maybe we should drop this whole subject."

"Yes, maybe." He stood up, frowned at her a moment, and then walked off with slow contemplative strides. Diana rolled onto her stomach and buried her face in her arms. Why couldn't she ever leave well enough alone? Why did she always have to go running headlong into other people's problems?

The answer wasn't hard to find. The truth was, she was as meddlesome as her brothers. They were all cut from the very same cloth. Only three weeks into the summer and already she felt too fond of the people at Cliff Haven, already too enmeshed in the everyday events of their lives. But she couldn't help it. That was just the way she was. Naturally she couldn't help feeling pain when they hurt. Neither could she keep from wanting to help.

But David didn't want her involved, and he certainly didn't invite her help. Perhaps because of his past, he trusted only himself to handle his affairs or those of his family.

Just then she felt the coolness of a shadow across her bare back. She swung around and looked up at David's towering figure. A tear trickled down her cheek.

He was about to say something when he noticed. "Aw, don't do that. Diana, for heaven's sake! I'm not mad at you." He thrust a hand through his damp hair. "It's me! How the *hell* could I let that happen? How could I lose touch with the people who mean the most to me?" His shoulders rose and fell with sharp angry breaths. Finally he lowered himself to the blanket. "Okay. I'll do what I can. As head of this poor excuse for a family, I guess I should. I'll make the time."

Diana rested her forehead against his shoulder. "Thank you."

"No. Thank *you*." He raised her chin and stared into her eyes. He was going to kiss her, she thought. Small candle-flames of desire were burning in his eyes, and his mouth had a serious hungry curve to it. But then he looked away, took a deep breath, and when he looked back, the moment was gone. He leaned across her and lifted his watch from the folds of his shirt. Suddenly an unexpected dread gripped her heart.

"What's up?"

"I have to catch a plane back to New York at six o'clock."

"Oh." That's what she'd suspected. "Well, that still gives us a couple of hours." She blushed almost immediately. What if he wanted to spend the rest of his time here alone— or, worse, with someone else?

"Mm, but I should be packing." He seemed hesitant. "What did you have in mind?"

She sat up, equally hesitant. "Would you care to go into town? There's always something to do there." She waited for his excuse, sure that he would make one.

David sighed thoughtfully. "Would you like us to take your car? You don't seem too crazy about my bike."

Diana was afraid she would laugh out loud in her relief. "No, your bike's fine. Much better actually. Parking's horrendous on Sundays." She got to her feet and tugged on her beach robe. Going into town with David would be so much fun. Suddenly there wasn't a moment to waste.

David seemed stiff at first as they explored the gift shops along the harbor, and Diana noticed he never took off his dark glasses. As for herself, she was having a ball. She'd walked through these very same shops several times before, but with David along, they seemed transformed. The afternoon was charged with a special excitement.

Later they strolled out to Christie's Landing for something to eat. A Dixieland band was playing, and people were dancing right on the wharf. They sat at an umbrella-shaded table and ordered lobster rolls and frosty mugs of beer. The surrounding waters were jammed with boats, from multimillion-dollar schooners to humble dinghies. The sounds of their horns and bells punctuated the air, enhancing the harbor's holiday mood.

Diana happened to glance at her watch as they were eating. Immediately she jumped to the edge of her seat. "David! It's quarter to six!"

He nodded, smiling his endearing, slightly crooked smile.

"Don't you have a plane to catch?"

"I think so," he answered calmly.

Of course, it couldn't mean anything, she told herself shakily. So what if David had decided to miss his plane? And so what if he was looking at her as if she were a large part of the reason?

He glanced away. "I...I'd like to stick around Cliff Haven one more day. See if I can talk to Evelyn about Cissy."

"Oh." Diana felt ridiculous for having assumed what wasn't there. "Oh, of course. Good." She had to remind herself that David had been seeing someone else for three years, someone who provided everything he wanted in a relationship. Why would he want to get involved with her? He didn't have the time or inclination for emotional involvements. For that matter, neither did she.

But the plain truth was that it was happening, anyway, whether she ranted against it or not. She was attracted to David to a degree that stunned her, and what was perhaps even more alarming, she was beginning to realize she liked him, too. She really liked him, liked doing things with him, liked sharing his company and conversation.

But how did he feel about her? What purpose was she serving in his life? Diana gazed at his dark chiseled features and wondered for the thousandth time what was going on behind those blue eyes.

He sipped his beer and leaned forward, staring at her with unnerving interest. "So, Diana—" the corner of his mouth lifted into that roguish smile she was learning to love "—as long as I'm going to be here..."

"Yes?"

"Have you ever been to jai alai?"

"No." She was becoming increasingly light-headed.

"Me, neither. And I was just thinking I'd love to go tonight. How about you?"

DIANA WAS IN an abstracted state all through Cissy's lesson the next morning. David's being home on a weekday was such a novelty. She watched the clock with mounting anticipation.

They'd had a wonderful time at jai alai. David had been hilarious, refusing to place even a two-dollar bet until he'd had a chance to watch a few games and size up the players. Diana, on the other hand, had exasperated him by picking her tickets from the numerals in her birth date. But when she won a fifty-four-dollar quinella, he'd tossed his program into the air in disgust and started betting her way.

Midnight had found them at a pancake house. By one they were home. He didn't kiss her, but she knew he'd wanted to. Ever since she'd told him about Ron and her fear of being hurt again, he'd held back. But she sensed it was a control that wasn't coming easy. He had to work at it, as she did, and she wondered if he had any idea how quickly her fear was disappearing, or how much she wanted him to forget his chivalrous concern.

She'd had lunch and corrected Cissy's work before David finally came over. "I really can't stay, Di. Already my secretary had to cancel a conference this morning." He stood by the door, hand on the latch.

"When will you be back?"

"I'm not sure."

Diana didn't know what to say. Thank you for a lovely weekend? Please don't go? She felt sad and confused. She glanced up and noticed that David looked just as distressed. Suddenly he pulled her into his arms and kissed her the way she had been hoping and dreaming he would ever since she'd asked him to stop. Only now, the reality far surpassed her dreams.

Finally he drew his head back and breathed a long shaky sigh as if he had felt something he hadn't counted on, either. Then with an effort he pushed himself away and stepped out to the stair landing. He didn't say anything else, just gave her one last smile that reached down to the deepest part of her, and was gone.

THE NEXT AFTERNOON, Diana was just coming back from hiking the Cliff Walk, a three-mile path that ran behind some of the grandest mansions in Newport, when Abbie came lumbering over from the main house.

"You have a letter," she called, waving the envelope.

Curious. Diana had received mail here before, from school, from her family, but Abbie's eyes had never looked so mischievous.

"It came by special courier."

"Thanks, Ab." She took the envelope and glanced at the return address. It was from David. Immediately her heart was thundering.

Upstairs, she dropped her purse and camera on the couch and tore open the envelope.

"Dear Diana," the typed letter began. It was on crisp company stationery. "Included with this letter you'll find a couple of tickets to the Newport Folk Festival, which is this upcoming weekend." Diana began to smile. "I noticed your collection of tapes last Sunday and came to the conclusion there's no type of music you don't like, which leads me to think you'll really enjoy the festival. I wish I could be there to enjoy it with you . . ."

Diana's eyes swam out of focus. *Wish I could be there . . . ?*

"Unfortunately I'll be in Atlanta. But I've called an old friend in Newport who says he'd be delighted to take you. His name is Stan Hillman."

David was setting her up with somebody else? She couldn't believe what she was reading.

"I thought you might enjoy getting to know someone in Newport outside our family. Stan's a terrific guy. He's thirty years old, teaches art history at a nearby college and drives a funky old Aston Martin. I have a feeling you two are really going to hit it off."

There was a hastily scrawled signature—and nothing more.

CHAPTER TEN

DIANA LOWERED HERSELF shakily to the couch and stared at the letter. What had happened? Hadn't David held her in his arms just yesterday? Why was he pushing her toward another man? And pushing it was. She could interpret it no other way.

Had he suddenly remembered she was just an employee? Had he decided she'd become too familiar with him and his family and had better transfer her interest somewhere else?

Perhaps he'd come to the conclusion she simply wasn't worth his time. If there was no chance of having an affair with her, as she had told him, why should he bother with the tiresome preliminaries?

Or was she just so pitiful that everybody who came in contact with her felt the need to arrange a blind date for her with the nearest bachelor?

Whatever had prompted this letter, Diana was certain of one thing: she'd been crazy to let herself get involved with David Prescott. She'd spent the past twelve months guarding so carefully against the possibility of being hurt again. Why, then, had she been so ready to throw caution to the wind with David? Had this fairy-tale place lulled her into believing that what happened here really didn't matter? Had this summer out-of-time tricked her into thinking the pain really wouldn't hurt?

She was still sitting there staring at the letter when her phone rang.

"Is this Diana White?"

"Yes."

"Hi, my name is Stan Hillman . . ."

Diana covered her eyes with an unsteady hand. "Oh, yes. I just got David's note."

"Good, that saves a lot of explaining." He had a nice voice, rich and melodious, and Diana wondered what he looked like. She hoped he was terribly unattractive. Then she'd know David had merely wanted her to have an escort to the festival.

"Diana, I hope you don't mind this. I mean, I don't usually let my friends arrange my social life, either, and if you'd like to call it off, I understand."

"Listen, Stan, I honestly don't know what I want to do. I haven't had much time to think about David's letter."

"If you want to know the truth, I didn't trust his call myself. I wondered if maybe you and he were an item and he was trying to get you off his hands."

Diana's spine straightened. "Why? Is that what he usually does when he gets sick of someone?"

Stan chuckled. "We've been known to come to each other's rescue upon occasion. But he assured me that wasn't the case this time. He said there was nothing between you. You were simply a guest in his house."

"I tutor his niece." Diana's throat was growing so tight she was surprised she didn't croak.

"Yes, and he feels concerned that you might be getting bored."

"Well, isn't that decent of him."

There was a pause. "Are you sure I'm not stepping on anybody's toes here?"

"Positive."

"Okay, that's the last time I'll ask. Now about Saturday . . ."

"The folk festival. Sure, I'd love to go with you, Stan." Though her voice was even and friendly, her right hand was crushing David's letter into a hard ball. A moment later she pitched it across the room. "Dinner Thursday? That sounds terrific... Fine. See you at seven." She hadn't the foggiest idea who this Stan Hillman was, but she was determined to have a ball. And David and his unpredictable mood swings could go straight to hell!

WHEN STAN STEPPED from his sports car Thursday evening, Diana was peeking out her window, chewing her nails. He looked up and she dropped her hand—and then her jaw. He was gorgeous!

Stan turned out to be a wonderful person, as well. He was so unlike David that she had trouble believing the two were friends. Where David was reticent and distrustful, Stan was outgoing and gracious. Even physically he was different, with his blond Robert Redford looks and dazzling smile. And one more thing—David was right; she and Stan hit it off immediately.

They had dinner at the elegant Sheraton on Goat Island and later retired to a top-floor lounge where they danced till midnight. Across the harbor, the boats and buildings of Newport seemed strung with fairy lights. She hated to leave but knew if she didn't get some sleep, Cissy's lesson tomorrow would be a waste.

The Newport Folk Festival, two nights later, was held on the grounds of Fort Adams, a formidable-looking fortification built in the early 1800s at the mouth of the harbor. Stan's and Diana's seats were perfect, dead center and six rows from the stage, but then she didn't suppose David ever settled for anything less.

The program started, and she was enthralled—but only for a while. She was dismayed to find herself thinking increasingly about David. She didn't understand why the blasted man still filled her thoughts or why her heart raced when his image crossed her mind. He obviously considered her just an encumbrance, someone he had to unload on a friend. And yet she couldn't free herself from thoughts of him. He wouldn't give her peace.

The concert passed in a blur and, before she knew it, was over. On the way home, Stan suggested they stop by his place for a drink. He wanted her to listen to a CD he had of one of the guitarists who had performed that night. Diana was beginning to feel that the only place she wanted to be was back at the carriage house, but it was Saturday night and perhaps too early to go home just yet.

Only when she was there did she realize what an imprudent decision she'd made. She was alone with Stan, in his apartment, and she didn't have any way to get home. And though he had been nothing but a gentlemen all evening, she knew she was, in a way, at his mercy.

He put on the CD she'd supposedly come to hear and fixed a couple of drinks. When he sat beside her, he sat very close.

"I really can't stay long, Stan."

"No problem. Whenever you want to go."

He was really a nice person, she told herself, and they were just doing what most other people did after a date. Still, she couldn't help feeling uneasy, the way she'd felt with every other man she'd tried to date that year. And instead of being flattered whenever he put his hand on her arm or leaned closer, she only felt an irrational urge to slap him away.

It didn't make sense. Stan was Mr. Perfect, yet something was wrong. She felt no attraction, no chemistry.

It was nearly one-thirty and he was insistently putting on another piece of music when the telephone rang. He swore under his breath as he yanked the receiver off the hook.

"Oh—hello!... Uh, yes, she's here... Yes, of course... No, that's not necessary... Honestly, David, you don't—" He held out the receiver and stared at it a moment before hanging it up.

Diana's heart thudded alarmingly. "David's home?"

"Sure is. Diana, are you certain there's nothing going on between you and him?"

She felt herself flushing. "Why would he arrange for you and me to go out if he and I...?"

"I don't know." Stan frowned. Then shrugging off the thought, he sat again, letting his arm drift across her shoulders. When he began to play with her hair, she'd had enough. She stood up.

"Stan, I've had a wonderful time—I really have—but I've got to go."

He looked offended. "Sure, but do you mind waiting a little while? David's on his way over."

Diana's strength drained. "He's coming here? Now?"

"Yes." Evidently it never occurred to Stan to say no to David. His concerned gaze traveled over her expression. "I thought so." He lifted her chin so that she had to look at him. "Oh, be careful, Diana."

She answered sulkily, "I know."

"Do you?" His eyes drilled into her. But before either of them could say another word, there was a buzz at the door. "Cripes! He must have phoned from the booth on the corner."

A moment later, David was standing there, and if Diana's pulse had been racing before, it was now completely out of control. As soon as he entered the room, his eyes sought her out and swept over her with an odd combination of hunger and concern. Then he smiled. Her face suffused with hot color as she smiled back. Almost as an afterthought, he said hello to Stan.

"I hope you don't mind my stopping by."

"Why should I mind? You were just in the neighborhood, right?" Stan's tight smile hardly disguised the irritation beneath it. "Would you care for a drink?"

"No, thanks." David's gaze returned to Diana, again roaming over her like a physical caress. It made her feel alive and utterly feminine.

She didn't have the vaguest idea why he had dropped in at a friend's at nearly two in the morning, but she was thrilled that he had. In fact, she could barely contain her sudden joy. It made no sense. For most of the week she'd been furious with him, but looking at him now, she realized his presence filled her senses, her spirits soared, and she forgave and forgot whatever had made her angry in the first place.

"I stopped by to see if I could save you a trip out to my place, Stan. As long as I'm here, I can give Diana a ride back."

Stan sipped his drink, eyeing David over the rim of the glass. "That's not necessary."

"I know, but it's the least I can do. You were nice enough to take her to the festival."

Diana's eyes flew from one man to the other. Competitive tension was crackling just beneath the surface of their politeness.

"I honestly don't mind the drive," Stan returned. "Actually, I'll rather enjoy it."

"I'll take her home," David said quietly.

Diana stood up and scooped up her purse. "Stan, thank you. I had a marvelous time. But David is right. I'll hop a ride with him and save you the trip."

Stan sighed and threw up his hands. "Okay, if that's what you want." And giving David a look of grudging admiration, "Take care, David, you hear?"

In silent accord, they hurried down the stairs. David handed her a helmet, mounted his bike, and waited for her to climb on behind. A moment later they were streaking down the road, Diana clinging to his waist and feeling distinctly like war plunder.

They roared through the night without speaking. The beaches and mansions whizzed by with the beautiful illogic of a surrealistic landscape. The wind whipped at her hair, but she wouldn't let go of David even to tuck it back.

The night was deafeningly quiet when he finally turned off the engine. They got off the bike and walked to the carriage-house steps. There they paused, standing so close she could see the spikes of color in his eyes. How she'd missed him! And how happy she was now! It was almost too much emotion to bear.

Suddenly she was in his arms without knowing how she got there, and he was lifting her off her feet in a fierce embrace. "Oh, Di! I thought this week would never end! It's so good to be home! How are you?"

She could barely speak for lack of breath. He set her down, and she nodded, somehow conveying that she was all right. He touched her lips, her cheek, her hair, smoothing its wind-whipped tangles. His eyes gleamed as they studied her. Then they both seemed overwhelmed by another flood of emotion. He pulled her close and kissed her. Her lips parted and matched his ardor with a fire of their own. Her hands slid under the silky warmth of his jacket and reveled in the hard strength of his back. His hands caressed her hips, drawing her closer, molding her to him. His kiss deepened until she moaned. When he finally released her, she felt airborne. She clung to him, her head resting under his chin, listening to his racing heart.

She had been warned to be cautious of David—she could never say she hadn't. But there was something at work here that was headier than reason, a force even stronger than her sense of self-preservation.

She shrugged from his embrace and took his hand. "Let's go upstairs." They climbed hand in hand and, at the top, closed the door against the rest of the world.

In the dim light of a small lamp, David gathered her back into his arms. Beneath the soft cotton of his shirt, he was whipcord lean and hard, and just the light touch of her palms brought a weakness to the pit of her stomach.

"I've been thinking of holding you like this all week," he murmured, brushing his lips over the crown of her head. "I'm sorry about this thing with Stan. Did everything go all right?" His voice was low and languid with desire.

She nodded, nestling closer. He scooped her up into his arms and walked to the couch. There he lay her down and sat beside her.

"Why did you do it, David? Why did you set me up with him?"

He looked away. "I thought it would be good if you met someone else who could take you out. But then, once it happened, the idea drove me crazy. I'm afraid I made a fool of myself tonight, barging in on the two of you like that."

Diana laughed softly. "Did you think I was being ravished?"

"Well, if anyone's got the moves, it's Stan Hillman. When you didn't come home right after the concert, I got worried."

"You're as bad as my brothers." She brushed a finger lightly over his firm thin lips. She'd never felt so complete or so at peace as she did now, locked within the world created by his concentration on her.

"Di, the real reason I arranged this date with Stan..." His brow furrowed. "When I left here Monday, I started thinking about the wonderful weekend we'd spent, and I got scared. I don't know how it happens, but when we're together, things get sort of crazy. I do things I never intended..."

"And that scares you?"

"To death. All my adult life I've worked at being independent and in control. That's all I've ever wanted. Am I making any sense?"

"I think so. I make you feel vulnerable."

He nodded solemnly.

"So you fixed me up with the nicest, most attractive guy this side of Mars, thinking I couldn't help but fall for him."

"I didn't mean to push you into anything you couldn't handle. I know what you went through last summer."

"You just wanted to push me away from *you*."

He stroked her face, the look in his eyes so tender Diana felt weightless. His head lowered and his mouth touched hers, gently, savoring the softness of her lips. Then he made his way to her eyes, kissing each lid as lightly as a breath. "Di, if he happens to call again, don't go out with him."

"I never intended to." The last syllables were all but smothered under the warm pressure of his lips. This time they parted hers with a hot insistence that sent her into a mindless tailspin. Soon all she wanted was to lose herself in the fire of his body.

But David surprised her by sitting up. "There's nothing I'd rather do right now than carry you off to the bedroom, but we both know that would be a mistake."

Diana lay beside him, trembling under the light touch of his hands on her arms. No, not a mistake, she wanted to say.

Making love with this wonderful man suddenly seemed the best, most natural thing to do, and she wondered why she'd never felt this way before, not even with Ron. And as she watched him watching her, the answer quietly entered her heart. She was in love with David. For the first time in her life, she was totally, madly, in love.

"Something wrong, Di?" he whispered.

"No. Yes." She didn't know whether to laugh or cry.

David pulled her into his embrace, his chest rumbling with laughter. "Exactly how I feel."

Was it? she wondered. Did he have any idea what she'd just discovered about herself? As much as she wanted to believe he was in love, too, she didn't dare. They'd grown close, but she was painfully aware that he still kept a guard on the innermost tickings of his life. And when two people loved, there were no secrets.

"I should go." He kissed her quickly and wrenched himself up from the couch. "I can't be compromising the reputation of the local schoolmarm now, can I?"

Be my guest, she thought, rising also. "No, I suppose not. Everybody's giving me strange looks as it is."

"I know what you mean. Do you have plans for tomorrow?"

"No."

"Want to sail out to Nantucket?"

"Sounds great."

"Good. See you around nine, then."

"Good night, David." His gaze washed over her and again she was a lost drowning woman.

THE ROCK MUSIC pulsing from Diana's radio wasn't having the effect she'd hoped. She still felt miserable. And confused. She dropped her sunglasses into the bag she was packing for the sail to Nantucket and then fell back on her bed. As soon as David had left last night, the reality of her predicament had set in, and she'd thought of little else since.

Falling in love was not what she'd set out to accomplish this summer. It was precisely what she'd wanted to avoid. She hadn't fully healed from the last disaster yet, had she? Where would she find the strength to survive another? And it *would* come, just as surely as the seasons changed and her days here in David's world would run out. But even if she and David did have endless time, he'd told her repeatedly he wasn't interested in a serious relationship.

Then what was all this running back to her on weekends? Why the jealousy over Stan? Was it just a physical hunger she'd aroused in him? She wanted to believe she'd touched him more deeply than that, that she'd somehow broken through the barricade he held between himself and the world, but she suspected she'd only be kidding herself if she did.

She sat up, admitting she had no answers.

She was stuffing a towel into her bag when the telephone rang.

"Hello?"

There was a slight pause, then, "Diana, are you all right?"

"Hi, Stan. Yes, I'm fine." She guessed her hello had been rather flat.

"No, really. How *are* you? I hardly got any sleep last night worrying about you. I never should have let David whisk you off like that. I'm sorry."

"I'm just fine." She tried to sound upbeat this time.

"Well, I hope so. You're too nice a person. I'd hate to see you get hurt."

She tensed. "What makes you think I might get hurt?"

"Because David is what he is—a user."

"Stan!"

"Don't get me wrong. He's a wonderful guy when he's in your corner. The best. It's just when it comes to women...well, you know. Ever since that incident with Glenda... We can all try to pretend it never happened, like he does. But it did, and it changed him."

Diana's heart seemed to constrict as Stan's words sank in. There had been an incident with Glenda? Walter's wife? From the offhand way Stan mentioned it, he evidently assumed the "incident" was common knowledge.

"I'm sorry, Stan, but you've lost me. I know he and his brother don't speak because of the disagreements they had settling their father's estate. But Glenda... I'm not sure I know which incident you're referring to."

"David's being dumped, of course. What else?"

Diana sank into the nearest chair. "Oh, that. Yes, of course."

Stan was quiet a long while. She wondered if her voice had conveyed any of the hysteria she was feeling.

"I'm sorry, Diana," he finally said in a low apologetic tone. "I thought you knew."

She was too embarrassed to say anything and the silence spun out.

"David and Glenda went together years ago," he explained hesitantly. "Actually, they were engaged."

David had once been engaged. He'd been that close to another woman? Diana trembled, realizing how little she knew about the man she loved.

"And... what did you say? *She* broke up with *him*?"

"Uh-huh. And married Walter instead. David's never been quite as, well, considerate of women since."

"Glenda," she repeated dazedly. "You mean she's the reason he doesn't let himself get involved with anyone?"

"Afraid so."

She hadn't seen a single picture of the woman anywhere in the house, nor had she heard any conversations about her. Yet this mysterious Glenda had once wielded such power over David that her leaving him had soured him forever on romantic involvement?

"She hurt him pretty badly, I take it."

"Yes, pretty badly."

"She must have been some woman."

"She...yes, she was. I've seen David go through lots of women since, but none of those relationships were nearly as serious."

That wasn't what Diana had wanted to hear. She blinked rapidly and tried to swallow the lump in her throat. No wonder David considered a reconciliation with his brother impossible. More stood between them than just a stolen steel empire.

"That's why I'm calling," Stan continued. "To make sure you don't become one more casualty."

"I appreciate your concern, Stan, but I'll be all right."

"I hope so."

"I will. I wish I could talk longer, but I really have to run."

"I won't keep you then. But do me a favor—don't toss out my number just yet, okay?"

"I won't."

Diana hung up the phone and gazed out the window. David was coming through the front door of the main house. "I'll be all right," she repeated in a shaky whisper, but she already knew she didn't believe a word of it herself.

CHAPTER ELEVEN

"...JUST THE WAY we did yesterday with 'Birches.' Let your mind float free through all the possible connotations of the image— Hold on!" Diana threw down her book and went to the window. "What *is* that racket?"

"Oh, Uncle David's having the gazebo repaired," Cissy informed her. "The floor's rotted in a few places."

"Really? And he's actually taken the time to notice!" Her voice grated as if David had planned the repair expressly to irk her. Ever since he'd left for New York three days ago she'd been in a foul mood. It had started on the drive to the yacht club Sunday morning.

"Awfully quiet today," David had commented. "Anything wrong?"

She'd shaken her head and looked out the window, sinking further into the sullen speculations that had begun with Stan Hillman's call.

David had then pulled to the side of the road. "Don't tell me there's nothing wrong. I've never seen you this quiet before."

"Everybody's entitled to a bad mood once in a while."

He'd flicked off the ignition and given her a look that told her they would be going nowhere until she talked.

"David, do you like me?"

"What?"

"Do you like me? Do you consider me a friend?"

He'd laughed. "Yes, of course."

"Then why is it you've never told me about Glenda?"

For the rest of her life, Diana was sure she'd never forget the look that had come over David's face. "The first time we met," he'd said icily, "I gave you a lot of orders. Most of them were silly and embarrassing, but there's one thing I'll never retract—don't go prying into my personal business!"

Diana had flinched. Lately she'd begun thinking she *was* his personal business.

"Damn it, Diana! Why are you so fascinated with my past? It's gone. Ancient history."

"Is it?" she'd accused. "Is it really?"

"And what's that supposed to mean?"

"It means I think the past is very much alive and festering inside you, David. Losing your mother, what Walter did, Glenda's defection. You won't let any of it go. Any of it. It's turned you bitter and distrustful and it's robbing you of a future, but still you won't let go." Diana hadn't realized she'd been harboring so many opinions, and as they'd poured out, she'd become almost as shocked as David. Still she'd continued, "You dwell on your anger, David. It's what drives you. To work like a madman. To succeed beyond anyone's wildest dreams. To make those who hurt you pay, with their envy and regret and—"

"Enough!" That one command had carried such menace she hadn't dared say another word. "I think we ought to forget sailing today," he'd muttered, turning the key so hard the ignition ground. Then he'd sped back to Cliff Haven, back to its locked gates and No Trespassing signs, and within an hour was gone.

Diana had seen him angrier but never quite as defensive. It reminded her again how little she really knew him—and how strongly he wanted to keep things that way.

"I'm glad it's being fixed," Cissy said. Diana shook her head, trying to remember what they were talking about. "In the past that gazebo was used as a bandstand at parties. There used to be lots of parties here, though I don't remember them, of course. They were all before I was born. But we have tons of old pictures."

Diana returned to the table. "Let's get back to Robert Frost."

Twelve o'clock came around slowly. Normally Diana loved tutoring, but since her argument with David, she seemed to have lost interest in everything. She had an unappetizing cup of yogurt for lunch and then forced herself to read a grant proposal Evelyn had written for an adult-literacy project she was involved with in New York. When she'd jotted down a few ideas of her own, she took the proposal over to the main house. It was Cissy who came to the door.

"Oh, hi! I'm glad it's you, Miss White. Come here." She took Diana's arm and hauled her in, through the foyer and into a receiving room. Stacked on the settee were several satin-covered books.

"These are the family albums I mentioned this morning. I love looking through them." She patted the seat beside her.

"I just came over to return something to your mother."

"Sure, but you *have* to see this. Aren't these outfits too much?"

Diana was curious. She sat and within seconds was hooked. The photographs were priceless, capturing an era the way no textbook ever could, from the Gilded Age, through the raucous twenties, right up to the recent past. Diana looked at them all, and what she saw was a summer home alive with activity and happy social gatherings. She also saw a warm fun-loving family, for generations back, that proud aristocratic beauty marking the features of every one. In fact, she saw too much.

David's youthful handsomeness was so poignant it brought a tightness to her throat. He was in dozens of pictures, horseback riding with his mother, sailing with his sister, helping Abbie's husband tend a clambake. As he grew into his teens, however, another person appeared with increasing frequency, a blonde with delicate porcelain features and huge cornflower eyes. Even from across the span of time, Diana could see they were very much in love.

She knew Cissy was watching her and had been for some time. "That's Glenda, my uncle Walter's wife," the girl finally said. "She went out with David first, before Walter. They were even engaged for a while."

Diana tried to contain her reaction but knew it was overwhelming her. "How old were they?"

"In that picture? I'm not sure. Young. They started dating at fifteen, broke up about six years later."

Fifteen. Diana hadn't realized all that trouble had occurred so long ago. "Do you have any idea what happened between them?"

Cissy shrugged. "One day Glenda decided she didn't love him anymore. Sad, isn't it? I'd just die if somebody jilted me like that." She lifted another album off the floor, a scrapbook filled with newspaper clippings. She flipped through the pages until she found the items she wanted. Without saying a word, she placed the album on Diana's lap and stood up. "Y'know, I haven't even had lunch yet. I get so engrossed."

"Cissy, no..." If David didn't want her poking into his background, he certainly wouldn't want her looking at these clippings.

"I'll be right back as soon as I've had a sandwich. Can I get you anything?"

Diana shook her head. She considered leaving, but as soon as the girl was gone, she began to read. She couldn't resist.

Just as old Doc Wilson back at school had said, the Prescott family had indeed been in the public eye. But the longest, most detailed articles always seemed to involve David—the plane crash, his romance with Philadelphia socialite Glenda Hughes, the bitter dissension and court battles between him and Walter, and finally Glenda's marriage. David was prominent in each account. Diana no longer wondered about his obsession with privacy. His youth had been a nightmare of publicity.

Throughout the years, the press had followed the vicissitudes of the Prescotts as if they were royalty. Everything they did was a new installment in an ongoing public saga, each generation providing a few new chapters. Evidently, by the time David and Glenda arrived on the scene, people were ready to perceive them as society's crowned prince and princess. Reporters followed them everywhere, ever hungry for a glimpse into their glittering privileged lives.

Diana thought her heart would break for David—or at least for the David she saw in these yellowed clippings. He looked so happy, this coltish nineteen-year-old on the slopes of Gstaad where he and Glenda had just announced their engagement. How much older he looked only two years later as he hurried down the steps of a New York courthouse!

Diana flipped the pages with mounting agitation. She had to find more about Glenda. What had ever possessed the girl to break up with David? And when, *when* had this actually happened?

Suddenly it was all there, right at Diana's fingertips.

"Diana? Are you still here?"

Diana wiped her eyes quickly. "Y-yes."

Evelyn entered the room hesitantly. "I see Cissy's been at the old albums again." She sat beside Diana.

"I hope you don't mind. I came over to return your proposal, and I got sidetracked."

"Of course not." Evelyn's smile faded, though, as she recognized the album on Diana's lap. She picked up a loose clipping—Walter and Glenda's wedding—and skimmed the print. "But the topic that dominated most conversations this afternoon," she read sardonically, "was the conspicuous absence of the groom's brother and sister." She shook her head sadly as she replaced the article.

"He was put through the ringer, wasn't he?" Diana said.

"David? Ah, yes."

"Glenda broke off their engagement after it became evident he wasn't the Prescott who was going to inherit the family's steel interests, right?"

Evelyn sighed. "Oh, she denied it to the end, but it was pretty obvious. Why else would she break up with David? He adored her, and he had so much going for himself. And to this day I still believe she loved him, too. But apparently not as much as she loved the Prescott fortune. As if that weren't bad enough, he had to suffer it all in the limelight of the press."

Diana hunched over the album, lost in speculation. *He adored her,* she repeated silently. *He adored her.* She could understand how being betrayed had made him bitter. But was it also possible that Glenda had left an emptiness in his life no one was able to fill? Suddenly, Diana panicked. After all these years, was David still carrying a torch for Glenda?

No. The thought was absurd. Not even David could be so singleminded of purpose. Could he?

Cissy entered the room just then, and in silent accord they let the conversation drop. Evelyn picked up one of the albums lying on the floor.

"Good heavens! Is that really me under that huge hairdo?" she cried, making room for her daughter on the settee.

Diana leaned in to better see a picture captioned Family Reunion, 1962. "Those people aren't all Prescotts, are they?"

"They sure are. Cousins, aunts, uncles."

"And I thought I came from a large family." Diana's smile faded as she remembered the people she'd left behind in Vermont, people who, unlike the Prescotts, still gathered to take pictures like these. But then, they hadn't been tested the way the Prescotts had, by tragedy, by greed and deceit.

Cissy expelled a sigh that seemed to come from her toes. "Gosh, I have relatives I don't even know. Why don't we ever get together anymore?"

Evelyn swallowed with difficulty. "Oh, probably 'cause Kate and Justin are gone. My grandparents—that's who we all had in common."

Cissy sighed again, probably recognizing a poor excuse when she heard it, and opened a different book.

"Which one's that?" Evelyn asked.

"The one with Grandma Kate's big gala—1924."

Diana leaned in again, full of curiosity, as Cissy turned the pages.

"I wish we could throw a party like that," the young girl said. "Just once in my life, a real dressy affair, with tuxedos and ball gowns and flowers everywhere."

Evelyn glanced up. "Celia Osborne, the day you trade in those blue jeans for a gown I'll eat my hat."

"But I would, for a party like that."

Her mother chuckled. "It's too bad sweet-sixteen parties aren't in style anymore. Your birthday would be the perfect excuse. It's probably the last chance we'll get, too, if your uncle goes ahead and sells Cliff Haven."

"But sweet-sixteen parties *are* back in style. Where have you been, Mom?" Cissy's sun-browned face suddenly beamed with hope. "Oh, do you think we could?"

"You know we can't. Your uncle would never allow it."

Cissy sank back, sulking for a moment. "But we don't know that for sure. He's been doing an awful lot of strange stuff lately. Let's call him. He's probably in his office right now."

"Oh, honestly! You can be the most exasperating creature!" But there was something in Evelyn's voice that betrayed a fascination with the idea. "Let's think this through first. For instance, who would we invite?"

"Well..." Cissy sat forward. "I'd like my friends from the yacht club and maybe a few girls from school. About ten in all. That's not many, is it?"

"No, but if I know you, the figure will double by sundown."

"You could invite friends, too. Actually, this could be your party. The fact that it's my birthday can be secondary. I won't even complain about the music if you get one of those awful ballroom bands."

"Ballroom bands! Who said anything about music?" Evelyn laughed. "Will you listen to us! We're talking about this as if it's actually—"

"A small party then?" Cissy pleaded eagerly. "With records for music and potato chips for hors d'oeuvres?"

Evelyn fell reflectively quiet. "That's hardly what my sixteenth was like. What an affair that was! I'll never forget the gown I wore. It was from Paris, Cissy. Paris!"

"That's it." Cissy jumped to her feet. "I'm calling Uncle David. We'll never know unless we try. On second thought, let's have Diana—I mean Miss White—call him. She seems to have a way with him that we don't."

Diana's heart leapt to her mouth. She hadn't seen this coming. Evelyn and her daughter had been so engrossed she'd begun to think they'd forgotten she was even there. "No, Cissy!" she cried, but the teenager was already dashing across the foyer to the library phone.

"Cissy, wait!" Diana sprang out of her immobility. "I can't ask your uncle—"

"Sure you can," Cissy insisted.

"But what'll I say?" she asked no one in particular. "What'll I do?"

It was too late. "Hi, Mrs. Slater? This is Cissy Osborne. May I speak to my uncle, please?... Yes, it's very important." She covered the receiver and giggled. "Oh, no! She's ringing the conference room, and uh— Oh, hi! Uncle David?... No, nothing's wrong. How are you?... No, this won't take long. Somebody wants to talk to you. Wait a sec." With that, she thrust the receiver toward Diana. "Here. He's really busy. Better not keep him waiting."

Diana's legs turned to rubber as she took the phone. How was she ever going to do this? Her heart still ached over his angry refusal to talk about Glenda, his shutting her out from that part of his life as if it were sacred territory, and he was undoubtedly still angry at her for her persistent meddling.

"David?" Her voice was high and thin.

"Yes...Diana? Is that you?"

"I know you're busy. I won't keep you long."

"That's okay. What's up?" His voice was hesitant, guarded. Still, Diana loved hearing it again. The timbre of it brought his face to mind distinctly.

Evelyn took her daughter's arm. "Cissy, let's let Miss White handle Uncle David alone."

Diana returned a smile of gratitude as they left the room. "David, I...we..." How was she ever going to ask his permission to throw a party at Cliff Haven? It went against every grain of his character. "David, your sister and I have just been discussing a matter that needs your approval. It concerns Cissy's birthday."

"Oh, yes, that's in August sometime."

"Right. In two and a half weeks. She'll be sixteen, David, and we were wondering if we could have a little party for her."

"Sure." He seemed to be shedding some of his wariness.

"But we were wondering if it could be a little more momentous than just a cake and ice-cream affair."

David's sigh crackled over the wire. "Exactly how momentous?" he asked suspiciously, but she could almost see the mocking glint in his eyes. She smiled through her trepidation.

"The details haven't been worked out yet but...oh, David, this would be such a great opportunity for Cissy and Evelyn to get to know one another again. There will be so much to do during the next two weeks they'll be forced to spend hours and hours together planning and shopping and whatnot."

"Hm, it's the whatnot that's got me worried. What exactly do you have cooked up?"

Diana couldn't believe how receptive he was being. Perhaps he was trying to make amends for storming off three days ago. "Well, basically it'll be an outdoor party in the late afternoon or early evening, fifteen or twenty guests. Of course there'll be refreshments, probably a buffet," she improvised, "and a little music."

"This is beginning to sound highly suspicious."

"We're not asking you to do anything except give your permission. Evelyn will handle all the details and expenses. If you really feel uncomfortable about it, you don't even have to attend." She paused, biting her lip. "Well, can I tell her it's on?"

David drew in his breath. "I don't know, Di."

"Please, David. Cissy is so excited. If you could see her face, you'd know how much it means to her. It'll hardly raise a ripple on the surface of your life, but to her and Evelyn it may be a turning point." She waited. She could hear him nervously tapping on a tabletop.

"Evelyn will arrange the whole thing?"

"Uh-huh."

"And you'll make sure there are no press releases, no society columnists?"

"Of course."

He sighed, long and deep. "I must be clear out of my mind, but all right. Tell her it's fine with me."

Diana laughed with relief.

"What are you laughing at, troublemaker?" he drawled in a low sensuous voice. "If this thing gets out of hand, I'm holding you responsible."

"Me!"

"Yes, you, you little witch."

"David, aren't you in the middle of a conference?"

He chuckled. "Yes. As a matter of fact, I am."

"Then you'd better go. And thank you. Cissy's going to be thrilled."

"Di, wait!"

"Yes?"

She heard the rustling sounds of movement, a door shutting, and then a sudden quiet.

"About last Sunday..."

She held her breath. "I know. You're sorry. So am I."

"You *are* a witch. Now you're even reading my mind."

They both laughed, and suddenly Diana knew everything was all right between them again.

"Not as well as I'd like. When will you be coming home?"

"Not fast enough." His voice was a heart-stopping whisper. "I'll see what I can do to trim my schedule, but the way it looks now, I won't be back from Japan till a week from Friday."

"Japan!" Diana sank into his desk chair. "Oh, David!" That's all she could say. She wanted to cry. Each time he went away, time seemed to shift into a slower gear, until now ten days seemed an eternity.

"My sentiments exactly. Di?"

"Yes," she choked out.

"Can you forgive me for being such a jackass?"

Diana felt tears gathering in her eyes. "There's nothing to forgive. I'm the one who went prying into a sensitive area. I had no right." She waited, hoping he would refute her and say she had every right, hoping he'd take the time to talk about Glenda. But he didn't.

All he said was, "And I had no right getting angry."

"Maybe," she began hesitantly, "we can talk about it when you return?"

"I think not. It's done. Let's forget it, okay?"

Diana frowned. "Sure."

"You understand, don't you? I'm sick to death of the past. I hate dragging it up. It's tiresome. It's boring."

She paused, believing that he did indeed hate dragging up the past, but not because it was boring. "Sure, I understand."

"Good. Well, I'd better get back to my meeting."

"Right. Well, have a safe trip, David."

"See you soon, Di."

Diana hung up the phone, quietly rejoicing over their having made up. Still, what did it mean? Was she any more certain now where this summer was taking her than she'd been before the call? Had he said anything to make her believe his feelings for her were anywhere near what hers were for him? Her smile faded. For all she knew she was still just playing at romance, riding a one-way train straight into heartbreak.

FROM THAT DAY ON, Cliff Haven buzzed with excitement. Cissy and Evelyn were constantly going off shopping together. Abbie was turning storage closets upside down looking for linens and silver that hadn't been seen in years, and James groomed the grounds from sunup to sundown. As for Diana, she seemed to be doing a little of everything.

They were all having a great deal of fun. Yet Diana was becoming wary. In no time at all, a simple buffet had mushroomed into a dinner. Single buds on each table blossomed into whole bouquets, and the music was a live five-piece band. She helped write the invitations and was alarmed when she counted thirty-two. And every day Cissy or Evelyn thought of someone else who would just die if left out. Now there was talk of renting a tent.

With so much going on, Cissy had trouble concentrating on her schoolwork. She talked about dresses and how to do up her hair, which, luckily, had grown in enough over the summer to style. She became inordinately jumpy, too. She bit her nails, dashed to the mail as soon as it arrived, fell on the phone whenever it rang, and on more than one occasion was overheard muttering, "I hope things turn out all right."

Diana sympathized, but she knew she had to bear down now more than ever. Cissy had worked very hard, so hard that she would probably finish everything before the party.

Still, she had a long exam to take, and Diana didn't want her to jeopardize all that effort at the last moment.

She heard from David twice that week, but each call only left her feeling lonelier and emptier. It was unfair that love could do that to a person, she thought. Each night, she crossed off another day on her calendar, then went to sleep wondering what she was going to do with all this love when he finally did come home.

Two days before the party, Diana was kneeling within the border of perennials that edged the courtyard when the family car came up the driveway. Actually the plants were so overgrown she hadn't realized they formed a border until James told her.

As soon as he'd heard about the party, he'd begun to trim and weed, but he was getting on in years and the grounds were too extensive for him. Diana didn't know if her efforts were making any difference, but she was giving it a shot, anyway.

As the car approached, she stood up, clutching the straw hat Abbie had plopped on her head. Her arms were sunburned and two fingers had poked through her gardening gloves. Suddenly her heart raced with joy. The car stopped alongside her, David got out and waved James on. Then he stood there, staring at her with a look capable of melting steel. His gaze slid over her dirt-smudged clothing and back up to her eyes, and his mouth lifted at one corner into that little smile she found so maddeningly sexy.

She hadn't seen him in almost two weeks, but never for a minute had he left her thoughts. She'd missed him so much it had become a physical ache. She had so much to say, but at the moment she couldn't get even a syllable past her lips. All she could do was run, arms outstretched, and leap into his embrace.

He held her tight. She could barely breathe, but she didn't care.

Slowly, he eased his hold. "That's the sweetest hello a man could ever ask for." His lips found hers in a long urgent kiss. "And getting sweeter by the minute." he murmured against her mouth.

How was this possible? she wondered vaguely. In his embrace less than a minute and she was on fire. She'd never known such desire for a man. But then, she'd never known such love, either. It was deep, abiding, all-consuming in its power.

"It's so good to have you home, David."

He swept her into his arms and effortlessly carried her up the carriage-house stairs. "Good to be home," he said, smiling devilishly as he kicked the door closed behind them. Then he kissed her with the hunger of a starving man. Slowly, still kissing her, he set her down on her feet and pulled her closer. Diana's head was spinning, her body turning to a river of heat.

How strange life could be! How wonderfully, awfully strange! When she'd first met David she'd considered him the coldest man she'd ever encountered.

She still had no illusions that this fire in him was love. He was a virile man who had certain obvious needs—but emotional need was not among them. He'd been scarred by too many events and by too many people, and he'd disciplined himself against intimacy so he'd never be hurt again.

Neither did she believe she still had a chance of getting away with her heart intact. She loved David far too much for that. She feared for herself, but right now the fear wasn't quite enough. She didn't care if she got hurt. Right now David was more important.

She ached as if the injustice he'd suffered in the past were her own. She wished she could lift the pain from his heart—

the dark shadow of the plane crash, the wound where Walter had thrust his greed-driven deceit—and leave him free to love again and be happy. But most of all, Diana longed to erase the memory of Glenda, the beauty he'd courted for six ardent years before she'd tossed him aside in favor of wealth. Diana held him close, trembling with the desire to burn away those evil haunting memories, yearning to set him free with the heat of her love—even if only for a little while.

"Di, what's the matter?" David cradled her head in his hands, his worried gaze taking in her expression.

"Nothing." Her voice wavered as she took his hand. He looked at her questioningly. She returned a small shy smile and then gave his hand a tug as she led him toward her room.

CHAPTER TWELVE

THEIR LOVEMAKING was exquisite torture. David took such gentle care with her, such slow pleasure, she almost couldn't bear it. She felt her whole life had been a preparation for this moment; her existence had no other reason. Every part of her, body and soul, ached to join him, to fulfill him and be fulfilled.

When it was over, she felt nerveless, as if she'd had an out-of-body experience and somehow found a way to remain there, floating among the stars. She reached for the sheet, drew it over them and, with a contented sigh, drifted into dreamless sleep.

She thought she'd awakened into an impressionistic painting, the afternoon light seemed that unreal. Beside her, David lay sleeping, his arm across her waist. His face looked peaceful and so much younger than she remembered. Trying not to wake him, she ran her fingers through the thick black silk of his hair, remembering how tenderly he'd made love to her an hour before.

His eyelids fluttered. He looked around with momentary confusion and a defensive tension that tugged at her heart. But when he realized where he was, he relaxed and smiled. His gaze melded with hers, enclosing them within the small private world they could create whenever they were alone together. "How are you doing?" he whispered.

She smiled dreamily, still finding it hard to believe she'd taken this momentous step. "I feel . . . wonderful!"

He nodded and smiled as if he understood.

"But scared, too, as if I've just stepped off into space."
She leaned up on one elbow. "What have we done, David?
What are we doing?"

He smoothed back her hair, a quiet intensity in his eyes.
"Having regrets already?"

"No. None. Never. It's only, well, we come from different worlds, and... and I'm not sure I know how to fit into
yours."

"That makes two of us then."

"I'm serious, David."

"So am I. If you're concerned about my family, or the
staff here, friends or associates, Diana, you get along with
them better than I do. You're personable and bright, and
you're genuine. You have a gift for fitting in."

She cast her eyes down and was quiet a moment. "Maybe
that's not what I was really asking." How was she ever going
to phrase this? How could she ask if she fit into *his* life?

"David, after I leave here..."

"Yes."

"We're never going to see each other again."

"Why not?" The corner of his mouth lifted. "Because of
a few hundred measly miles?"

Diana lay very still, afraid to break the spell of this magic
moment. He wanted to keep seeing her? Was he actually
saying they had a future?

David sat up, pulling her with him, and propped the lace-
edged pillows behind him. "So, tell me, Diana White, bane
of my life, what's been happening around here while I've
been gone."

Diana nestled into the warm crook of his shoulder, feeling incredibly happy and content. She told him all about the
party and how it had grown. She didn't want to keep anything back. When she mentioned that a tent had been raised,

he slipped from between the sheets and went to the window.

"Good Lord, it looks like a circus has come to town!"

"We didn't know what else to do, David. What if it rains?"

He turned, sunlight playing over his bronzed muscle-corded body, and he smiled one of his endearing crooked smiles. "So, what other damage have you done?"

"The fountain out back is working again. Oh, and I painted the gate. Did you notice?"

"You did that? I suppose you're the one who pulled up the Beware of the Dog signs, too?"

"Oh, David, I couldn't leave those horrid things there. What a way to greet guests!"

The mattress gave with his weight as he sat beside her. "This is going to be some bash, isn't it?"

"Afraid so."

"Are you going?"

"Yes. You?"

"Looks like I have no choice."

Diana bit her lip. "Are you angry?"

"Angry? No, just terrified."

"It's only a bunch of teenagers. Some family and friends. No one to get nervous over. I wrote out the invitations myself." But even as she spoke, Diana realized how glib she sounded. For David, a party at Cliff Haven undoubtedly set off emotional echoes that even she couldn't fully understand.

He pulled on his pants brusquely and sat down again. "You were right, you know. The last argument we had, you were right about my living in the past. I do. Or at least I used to. It gave me a reason, an order..." His voice thinned. "But I get the feeling everything's slipped out of control this summer. I've lost my grip..."

"Good," Diana whispered.

"Maybe." He stroked her cool bare arm. "But what did I expect, letting you into my life, hm? First time we met, you blinded me, crippled me, brought me to my knees." Grinning wickedly, he pushed her back into the soft pillows and leaned over her. Diana smiled with the realization that he wasn't brooding on the past anymore—or on anything else for that matter. He kissed her, and kept on kissing her, until neither of them was thinking about anything but making love again.

EARLY THE NEXT MORNING, a landscaping crew arrived. Cissy was sitting at Diana's kitchen table, engrossed in her final exam. Diana's heart went out to the girl. She was so nervous her hands were shaking as she wrote. Diana put down the book she was reading and went to the window. David and Evelyn were out there, talking to the men.

"Well, I'll be!" she whispered. So David was getting into the swing of things, too. But then she'd already sensed his mood changing last evening as they'd walked the grounds. Standing at the fountain, watching the setting sun enflame the tumbling water, she had almost heard his pride kicking in.

Diana instructed Cissy to leave the exam on the table when she was done and ran down to meet them.

"How's everything shaping up?"

"Good morning, Diana," Evelyn said, her eyes shifting from Diana to David with a merry twinkle. "I thought we were doing just fine until David stuck his two cents in. I told him it was too late, but do you think he listens? He's brought fourteen men to work on the grounds. Fourteen! And inside we have eight more washing windows and—"

"You only have yourself to blame. You started it. I'm just making sure it's done right." His eyes crinkled as he looked at Diana.

"So—" she smiled back "—what can do? I'm free for the rest of the day."

Diana ran errands all that morning. David, who had been helping the landscapers, joined her for lunch. Then together they carried china and crystal from the pantry out to the tent. Much to everyone's dismay, a heavy drizzle began to fall.

"This looks more like a wedding than a birthday party for a sixteen-year-old," he complained.

Evelyn ignored him as she continued to count place settings. "I hate to say this, Diana, but we could use one more table."

"Do you have any more?"

"We should. Out in the stable." Evelyn seemed tired, but as time-consuming and expensive as the party had turned out, it had done wonders for her relationship with her daughter.

"I'll go take a look."

"Would you? David, go with her and help. Four more chairs, too, please."

The air inside the stable was close and dusty. Yet the beauty of the building shone through—the clerestory windows, the intricately lathed posts of the stalls. It was a pity that David was going to sell Cliff Haven, but Diana supposed she understood. While it contained the best of his memories, it also contained the worst. This estate was his most tangible link to the past. Cut this . . . and he was free! Still, it was a pity.

They found the tables and chairs up in the otherwise empty loft. But David didn't seem in a hurry to carry them down right away. Instead, he stepped to the two haymow doors and pushed them open. A tide of misty light swept past him. He lowered himself to the floor and rested against the door frame.

"This is a lovely view. You can see all of Cliff Haven from here." Diana could tell that he was trying to speak without emotion, like the person he had been at the beginning of the summer, but he failed miserably.

Gingerly, Diana sat opposite him. Her gaze roamed over the estate, out to the muted gray sea. When she looked back, she was startled to find David's eyes on her, so still, so serious!

"Di, do you like it here?"

"Yes. Very much." She held her breath.

"So do I." With those few words she knew years of denial had just been reversed. "I think I'll hang on to the place a while longer. Besides, the interior of the house really needs an overhaul. I shouldn't try to sell it the way it is. What do you think?"

"That . . . that would be wonderful." Her throat was so tight with joy, her voice was barely audible.

His eyes traveled over her face, down her body to her legs, which she'd crossed at the ankles. A mixture of admiration and wistfulness filled his expression. "Di, talk to me," he said.

"Talk to you? About what?"

"Anything. I just love to hear your voice."

Diana cleared her throat. She paused, then cleared her throat again. For once in her life, she couldn't think of a single thing to say. She smiled diffidently.

"You know, you have a beautiful smile. It's so unaffected and warm. I bet you're going to have the loveliest lines in your face when you're old."

Diana looked down at her nervously interlacing fingers. She had made love with this man only yesterday, yet now she felt shy and a little frightened—as if they were on the edge of something immense.

"Di, I know I'm a difficult person to be with sometimes, and I know my work has . . ."

From where she sat, Diana could see the front gate open. A moment later, a car came up the drive. David looked out, too, and whatever he was about to say was momentarily forgotten. The car came toward the house so slowly it looked positively hesitant.

"Can that be the florist already?" Diana asked.

"I doubt it. Unless he's taken to driving a Mercedes lately." David's forehead puckered.

The car glided to a stop under the portico, and after a tense moment, two people got out. From the driver's side emerged a tall man with graying hair dressed in a light summer suit; from the other, a blonde who seemed to have stepped off the cover of *Vogue*.

"Oh, Lord!" David whispered, ashen under his tan. "Oh, dear Lord!" He trembled before his color came surging back. He leapt to his feet.

"David, what's the matter?" Just watching him, Diana was in a panic.

But he didn't answer and she suspected he hadn't even heard her. All he did was stare at the couple, as he stood there poised like a tiger about to pounce from his perch.

She turned and looked at them again, and suddenly awareness of who they were jolted through her. "That's your brother and Glenda, isn't it?" But David was still wild-eyed, breathing hard.

The couple walked to the front door, looking around slowly. Before they had a chance to knock, Cissy opened the door and let them in. Diana glanced at David. A vein was throbbing along the side of his taut face.

"Isn't that the strangest thing? Did you know they were coming?" Immediately she felt foolish.

He wheeled around and glared at her. His eyes, so loving just a minute ago, were now like hot coals, burning with the blackest anger she'd ever seen. Her nerves shattered.

"How could you do this to me? Diana, why did you invite them here?"

"But I didn't!"

"What did you tell them?" he went on, deaf to her. "We couldn't have a party without their hallowed presence?" His words came out stark and tight, through teeth that wouldn't unclench.

"But, David, I didn't!" She was so stunned by his accusation, she could barely speak.

"How could you do this to me?" he repeated, slamming the wall with his fist.

"David, please! I—I'm as surprised as you are."

He glowered down at her. "Are you? Well, somehow I find that hard to believe." He paced the floor, clenching and unclenching his fists as if he wanted to hit something again. "Damn it! Damn it!"

Watching him, Diana thought he looked rather like an animal pacing in a cage. Was he afraid of seeing Walter again, the brother who had shamelessly cut him out of his rightful inheritance?

Or... or was it Glenda? Was she the cause of this emotional maelstrom in David's soul? Diana's blood ran cold. Recently she'd wondered about David's feelings for Glenda—if he still carried a torch for her, deep down in some secret part of himself. But whenever the thought reared its head, she just as quickly denied it.

What a fool she'd been! What a stupid blind fool! Glenda was the first woman he'd ever let himself love, and he had loved her completely. "Adored her" were the words Evelyn had used. Glenda was also the only woman who'd ever been able to hurt him. Now as Diana stared at David, she realized that after all these years, David still loved his brother's wife. After all these years he was still open to being hurt by her.

David stopped his pacing and cast Diana a bitter look. "Why did I ever let you talk me into this damned party? You've changed everything. Why did I ever let you in here?"

Diana's throat constricted painfully. She couldn't believe how unfair he was being. Evidently the intimacy they'd shared meant nothing to him. One turn of events, and he was ready to hate her. There *was* no life for them in the future. The idea was absurd—and always had been. The only thing that loomed in her future was heartache and loneliness. David wanted no part of her, and never had. Not seriously.

Well, if that was the position he was determined to take, there was no use in trying to defend herself. There wasn't enough time left to the summer to do that. All she could do now was try to escape with a little of her dignity intact.

She stood up, straighted her back and lifted her chin. "I think I'd better go."

"Don't bother!" There was only contempt in his voice as he headed for the stairs.

"David, you aren't going to cancel Cissy's party because of this, are you? She'd be crushed if you did. She's been planning it for weeks, night and day."

"Looks like she wasn't the only one who was making plans." He turned stiffly and retraced his steps. "Do you think this is funny?" he said, pointing toward the car under the portico. "Do you think some miracle is suddenly going to happen? A great dramatic spirit of forgiveness embracing us after all these years?"

"No." Diana lowered her eyes. "But . . . but it would be wonderful if it did. I think you care about Walter more than you know."

"You poor deluded optimist!" His face was as dark as the clouds pressing down from the sky. "Diana?"

She looked up. "Yes?"

"Leave me alone. Please, get out of my life and give me back my peace."

He descended the stairs, his posture wooden and erect. Diana slumped against the wall and listened to him go, her lips trembling uncontrollably.

She watched him cross the courtyard through the drizzle, walking with the purposefulness of a man heading into a duel to the death.

I didn't do it! I didn't ask them here! she wanted to cry out. But he glanced up at her, standing in the hayloft door, and his cold blue eyes executed her on the spot. Her mouth closed and she lowered her head.

CHAPTER THIRTEEN

DIANA CARRIED the table and chairs to the tent, then hurried to the safety of her apartment. But even there, she was pursued by misery. With trembling hands, she set a kettle of water on for tea and forced herself to correct Cissy's exam.

When she was finished, she sat back and thought, well, at least there was one thing to redeem the summer—the girl had passed English with an A. Diana longed to tell her the good news, but she wasn't about to trek over to the main house now. She didn't even have the courage to phone. Heaven only knew what was going on over there or what kind of reception she would get.

With the test corrected, her summer here was done. She had nothing left to do. Nothing, that is, except think about David's unfair accusations and try not to cry. She loved him, more than she'd ever loved anyone in her life, and it destroyed her to be despised in return.

Early in the evening, there was a knock at her door. It was Abbie, florid-faced with excitement.

Diana jumped from the chair where she'd been nervously watching the house. "Abbie, what's going on?"

The old woman rolled her eyes and fell into a chair. "We were all trying to listen from the back hall, but it was hard. There was so much hollering going on."

"They're quarreling?"

"Oh, yes! And poor Celia, curled up in a chair like a mouse in the middle of them all."

Diana moaned. "What's going to happen?"

"I don't know. But if the roof don't blow by tonight, it never will." Abbie tried to laugh but the gravity of the situation defeated her.

"Do you have any idea why Walter and Glenda showed up—*now* of all times?"

"They say they got an invitation to the child's party! Can you imagine! They thought it was from Evelyn, and they figured if she could put aside her pride and invite them to a party, the least they could do was bring the girl a gift. They weren't planning to stay much beyond that."

"But Evelyn didn't send them an invitation. I helped her write them myself." She paused. "Oh, Abbie! You don't suppose..."

"That's just what I've been thinking."

"So that's why she's been so jumpy lately. Cissy took it upon herself to send them an invitation in secret! I bet she thought if she got them all together, she could force a reconciliation."

Abbie nodded vigorously. "But if she did, she hasn't owned up to it yet. For some reason, David seems to think you did it. I heard your name mentioned a few times."

Diana closed her eyes and fought back angry tears. "Well, if he insists on blaming me, that's his problem. If it'll keep Cissy out of hot water, I won't try to alter his verdict, either. He's not worth the effort." Diana felt Abbie's keen old eyes on her. "Well, he isn't!"

"Don't give up now, child. You've brought him so far. He'll come around."

Diana shook her head. "Not this time."

"Why do you say that? What's happened?"

Diana thought back to the argument in the stable and the words that had hurt so much. She was also aware of the person whose arrival had prompted those words.

"Abbie, do you think it's possible he's still in love with Glenda?"

Abbie's eyes narrowed. "You know all about that, do you?"

She nodded. She hoped the woman would reply with a ready "Of course not." But she didn't.

"Who can tell? He keeps so much to himself. I don't *think* he loves her. It's been so long."

"But you're not sure..."

"All I know is he loved her once. But she's no good for him. And he's aware of that."

Diana had her answer. But then she'd known it all along. She'd read it in David's face when he'd seen Glenda arrive. She was an obsession with him. She crowded out any possibility of new love ever blooming. Nobody else had a chance.

"The thing to do now is sit tight," Abbie said compassionately. "He still has some anger to work out. But then he'll come around. You'll see."

But Diana had no intention of sitting tight. He didn't want her in his life and never had. Well, she was determined to grant him his wish.

She went to the window dozens of times after Abbie left. The house looked still from the outside, but inside... She didn't want to think about what might be happening inside those thick stone walls. Lights went on, one by one. Then around ten o'clock, the caretaker came out to the Mercedes for a suitcase, and when Diana went to bed at twelve, the car was still under the portico.

SHE COULD TELL it was going to be a perfect day as soon as she lifted her bedroom shade. The drizzle from the day before had washed the world clean. Now the air was hot and dry, and a lovely evening was sure to follow.

Diana surmised the party was still on, in spite of the latest turn of events. Voices drifted from the service side of the house, and on the back lawn, caterers were dashing in and out of the tent.

She went to her closet and pulled out her luggage. She had wanted to attend the party so much, but there was no possible way she could do that now. With an aching heart, she began to pack her clothes. Why she hadn't started last night was beyond her. Maybe she'd been secretly hoping Abbie was right, that David would come over and apologize, talk to her and set everything right between them.

But he hadn't, and now she couldn't pack fast enough. It was time to get out of here, time to return to reality and get on with her life.

She was making her second trip down to her car when Cissy came jogging over. "Hey, what are you doing?"

Diana couldn't meet the girl's eyes. "I don't like to leave things for the last minute. Oh, hey! Happy birthday, sweetheart."

"Thanks. I can't believe I'm finally sixteen!"

"It's a landmark year, kiddo." Diana winked. "By the way, I've corrected your exam. You got an A!"

"An A!" Cissy threw back her head and laughed. "Now the day's perfect. Thanks, Miss White. You've been great."

"So, how is everything else—at the house I mean?"

Cissy grimaced. "Quieter than last night."

"Was it you who sent that invitation?"

Cissy's eyes lowered and she nodded. "I thought the feud had gone on long enough. I wanted the family to be together at my party." She flicked a worried glance over to the house. "I never expected the reunion to be easy, but, cripes, I never thought it would be this hard! I was sent to bed around midnight and they were still going at it!" She sighed wearily. "All I wanted... Well, our family used to be so big once, and happy—like yours—and I guess I just wanted a little of that for myself. Things are better today. I'm still in hot water, but at least everyone's agreed to overlook it till the party's over.''

"*You're* in hot water?"

"Mm. I wasn't going to say anything about sending the invitation, but somehow Uncle David got the idea you'd done it. I waited almost three hours before I did confess, though. I'm sorry."

"Don't apologize. It doesn't matter what David says or thinks about me. And another thing, don't let him bully you. Your intentions were noble. You acted out of the goodness of your heart."

"That's what Mr. Thorndike says, too."

"Emmet? Is he here?"

"Uh-huh. He arrived early this morning."

Diana couldn't help noticing the look of gratitude on the teenager's face when she mentioned Emmet as an ally.

"I guess he's not such a bad guy, after all," Cissy continued. "Oh, I haven't told you the biggest news of all—I won't be going back to Fairview in September."

"What!"

"Isn't that something? My mother wants me to stay home and help her get adjusted to married life. I'll be attending a school in New York just a few blocks from our apartment."

"Well, that certainly is something!" Diana began to smile. How clever of Evelyn to come up with such a brilliant rationale. "I'll miss you, kid. Fairview won't be the same."

"I'm sure it'll survive. Well, I gotta go. Gotta get my hair done. See you tonight, Miss White."

Diana waved with a too-bright smile, realizing it was probably the last time she would see the girl.

Packing took longer than Diana expected. She'd accumulated so much junk over the summer. And then she still had to run into town to pick up Cissy's gift at the jeweler's. She'd ordered a silver chain and a charm in the shape of a whale—to remind Cissy forever of her least favorite novel. She would leave it wrapped on the kitchen table along with a note apologizing for her hasty departure.

She'd just returned from running this errand when she glanced out the window and noticed David and Glenda stepping out of the house. They were already dressed for the party, David in a formal black suit, Glenda in a watery champagne silk dress. Diana hadn't realized it was so late. She should have been gone hours ago.

With troubled eyes, she watched them descend the stairs. Glenda was looking up at David and talking animatedly, a smile brightening her beautiful face. Whatever she said made him laugh.

They stopped at the Mercedes for a shawl. David took it from her and carefully draped it over her shoulders. Then they continued on their stroll, oblivious to the bustling preparations all around them.

Diana's insides felt as if they were being ripped to shreds. How many times had those two walked these grounds when they were young and in love? What was to say they weren't in love still? Maybe Glenda realized she had made a mistake in choosing the older brother. Maybe that's what she was telling David now.

Suddenly Diana feared for David, feared a situation that could easily break open into another public scandal, possibly the worst yet. As successful as he had been in downplaying his image over the past thirteen years, there would be no escaping the attention he'd provoke if he chose to pursue his brother's wife. It would be one more installment in the continuing Prescott family saga, moving with satisfying predictability toward the union of their two most glamorous characters. The press wouldn't be robbed of such a fairy-tale story, nor the innumerable spin-off articles that would mawkishly recount the events from the past that had led up to it.

But there was nothing Diana could do about that now. David was a grown man, with a will of his own. If he wanted to go after Glenda, then he obviously considered her worth the consequences. Besides, Diana had to think of a way to get out of here without drawing attention.

But in spite of her growing sense of urgency, she continued to lean on the sill, watching. Cars were pulling into the courtyard, and elegantly dressed people were converging on the back lawn. Orchestra music drifted on the breeze, now loud, then soft, and mingled with fragments of conversation and laughter.

For a moment, she heard David's voice above the others. She searched the gathering and found him, looking every bit the congenial host. What a change from the man she'd met only seven weeks before! He was devastating in dark evening clothes, tall, confident and so at ease. And why not? Glenda, the woman he had chosen to marry years ago was back in his life and smiling at him just a few feet away.

Diana could take no more. She knew what she had to do, and it had to be done immediately.

WITH HEADLIGHTS OFF, she inched her Toyota up the drive, through the gauntlet of cars parked along each side. Behind her, Cliff Haven was a blaze of lights. Music filled the air.

Her duties were over, she told herself, trying to put things into perspective. She had come here to tutor Cissy Osborne, and she had done her job—quite well, too. In the process, she'd put some distance between herself and her brothers, and she'd sailed right on by the anniversary of her almost-wedding without even realizing it. There was no earthly reason to stay in Newport any longer.

Out of habit, her foot moved to the brake as she approached the gate. What a tedious chore that had been—all that stopping and starting and getting in and out of her car just to pass through. But tonight the gates stood wide open and unguarded.

Suddenly she remembered her key. It was still in her handbag! She stopped the car and thought about returning to the carriage house to leave it on the kitchen table, but she didn't want to risk being seen and questioned. Then she thought, wouldn't it be a pleasure just to fling it into the woods! She dug the key out of her bag and stared at it. Slowly she touched it to her lips. No, she wouldn't throw it away. She would keep it as a souvenir and in years to come perhaps have it mounted. "Found art," she would call it, and when someone asked, she'd tell them all about the fairy-tale mansion with its locked gates where she had worked one timeless summer when she was young.

Where she had worked? And what would she tell them about all the love?

She sped up Ocean Avenue as if pursued. In the distance, far out on the promontory, Cliff Haven blazed on. Diana felt empty, empty of everything that really mattered. It was as if she had left her soul behind.

CHAPTER FOURTEEN

THE LAST TIME Diana had phoned her brother Skip, he'd been in the midst of packing for a camping trip. That had been four days ago, so she wasn't surprised to find the farmhouse deserted when she arrived, and the front porch light set on an automatic timer.

She carried her bags into the living room, then sank into an easy chair, letting her gaze roam over the quiet room. She hadn't told Skip that her job was ending a week ahead of time. She hadn't wanted him to change his plans just to be here when she returned, and she knew he would have, too. But now, how she wished she had told him. She needed a strong sympathetic shoulder tonight.

She'd left here thinking she didn't want or need that close familial concern, but she'd been wrong. That was not what independence was all about. Her family's concern had helped her weather so many storms. Even the stupid blind dates they'd arranged after the disaster with Ron had probably helped. They'd forced her to dress up, get out and socialize, and climb out of her occasional depression. Having observed the Prescotts, she now knew she was blessed to have family who cared enough about her to drive her crazy! How awful to have to go through life alone.

But then, she'd probably known that all along, she thought, recalling that the first change she'd made at the carriage house had been the installation of a telephone. No sooner had she arrived than she'd wanted to hear a familiar loved voice. And she had. She'd called everyone, once or twice a week throughout the summer—brothers, sisters-in-law, aunts, uncles. In fact, the phone had become her biggest expense.

She rose, suddenly wanting to call Andy or Mark to let them know she was back. But it was after midnight, and she would undoubtedly be rousing them from sleep.

She paced restlessly. By now the party at Cliff Haven would be long over, and everyone there would know she was missing. She hoped they weren't too angry. She would have to call tomorrow and say her goodbyes properly.

She wandered through the dining room, into the kitchen, flipping on lights as she went. Somewhere she would find comfort within these rooms, among the portraits and knickknacks and overstuffed furniture of her growing-up years.

But all she found was herself, alone. Tonight everything looked unfamiliar. The house had lost its sense of home.

She climbed the stairs to her old room, exhausted and eager to crawl into bed. But even as she pulled back the covers, she knew sleep would elude her. Her mind and heart were too full of Cliff Haven and how it had come to feel like home.

But of course it wasn't Cliff Haven. It was the fact that David was there. She knew she would feel at home wherever he was.

Why had she done it? she asked herself as she lay staring at the dark ceiling. Why had she fled Newport so abruptly? Was she that angry at him for distrusting her? Was she that hurt over his blind obsession with Glenda? That scared of hearing the words "I'm sorry, Diana, it's been fun, but…"?

Yes, she admitted, a resounding YES to it all.

Not that running away had provided an escape. The pain had followed her home, and as she'd suspected, it was far worse than anything she'd ever suffered before. But staying in Newport would only have made things harder. At least this way she'd preserved a modicum of pride.

Besides, it was too late for regrets. She'd done it. She'd left, and David was finally a part of her past, as she'd always known he would be. All she had to do now was figure out how to pick up the pieces of her life.

SHE AWOKE LATE the next morning. Someone was ringing the front doorbell. She hopped out of bed and threw on her robe, wondering if one of her brothers had been passing on his way to church and seen her car.

She peeked out the window and found, not one of her brothers, but a stranger in a uniform. Out in the driveway was a florist's delivery truck. She wiped her smudged mascara and opened the door.

"A delivery for Miss Diana White."

"Thank you." She took the long white box and turned.

"Ma'am? If you'll just wait..."

With stirred curiosity, she watched the delivery man return to his truck. He came back with five more identical boxes.

"Are you sure these are all...?"

"Yes, ma'am."

Stupefied, she waved goodbye and stared at the mysterious boxes stacked on the hallway floor. Almost fearfully she lifted one of the covers. Inside, nestled in green tissue, were a dozen perfect long-stemmed red roses. A card identified the sender simply as "David." Immediately her eyes filled with tears.

She opened the second box to find another dozen roses, the third box and the fourth—until finally six dozen roses scented the air with their heady perfume. She sank to the floor in the middle of them all and clutched her arms tight, holding back a sob. Why couldn't David let her make a clean break? Why did he have to prolong the suffering? Did he actually think that flowers would ease the pain of his dumping her? Did he think he could appease her with a consolation prize?

She picked up a few velvety buds and shakily breathed in their fragrance. She had never seen so many beautiful flowers in one place before. Except at funerals. How apt, she thought, as a tear slipped down her cheek. How perfectly, horribly apt!

Afraid that she was on the edge of completely breaking down, she hauled herself up and took the roses into the kitchen. Best to keep busy, she told herself, as she searched the cupboards for her largest vases. But as she worked, her mind inevitably returned to last evening's party.

As hard as she'd tried, she still couldn't shake the image of David, talking to his guests, with Glenda just an arm's reach away. He'd looked so at peace with himself—as if he'd finally come home to the person destiny had always intended him to love. Even from a distance she'd seen the change in him. Something of his old self was back, the youthful openness and charm, the expectant alertness in his features, as if the most wonderful thing was about to happen.

Diana set a vase in the middle of the dining room table and paused, staring unseeingly at the blooms. No one could fight Glenda, least of all a Vermont schoolteacher just passing through David's life for a summer. Glenda was an ideal of his youth, an ideal grown into obsession.

If only she'd known what she was up against, maybe she would have guarded her heart more carefully. But she hadn't. She'd let herself be carried away, by her surroundings, by David's passion, by her own eternal optimism. And now she was paying for it. Would she never learn?

She was just returning to the kitchen to fill yet another vase when the house began to vibrate with a loud clamor. She stopped in her tracks, startled, as the noise grew louder. Soon it was thunderous, banging on the windows and setting the jars in the spice rack to rattling. "What in the world?" she whispered.

She ran to the front door to see what was happening, only to be thrown back by the sting of wind and sand. She ducked inside again and chose to investigate from behind a closed window. What she saw made her mouth drop. There, right on the front lawn, was a small helicopter, its rotors slicing the sunny August morning with slowing revolutions.

Then she noticed the tall raven-haired man at its controls, and the morning became a bright swirling blur. David leapt down to the lawn and strode up to the front door without the slightest hesitation in his gait. He flicked a glance at the address, then rang the bell.

Diana fell back against the wall clutching her racing heart. What was she going to do? What should she say? But her mind was in such a fever she couldn't think. All she could do was open the door and stare up into David's arrogant sun-bronzed face—the most wonderful face she had ever known.

He didn't say anything at first, either. He just looked at her grimly, his shoulders rising and falling with his angry breathing. Then, "Diana, what the hell do you think you're doing?"

She reared back. "Well, good morning to you, too."

He brushed past her and stepped into the hall. "That was some stunt you pulled last night. Very dramatic!"

His attitude stung and brought her to life. "Oh, really! I didn't think you'd notice." She lifted her chin as defiantly as she could, aware of still being barefoot and dressed in a nightgown and robe. She hadn't even combed her hair.

But then, it didn't look as if David had gotten around to shaving, either. His hair was in disarray and he was wearing his worn jeans and a plain white T-shirt. He reminded her a lot of the man she'd met seven weeks ago outside the gates of Cliff Haven, a man trying to act tough and in command, even while suffering near-total incapacitation.

"And what's that supposed to mean, you didn't think I'd notice? Everybody noticed! You had a lot of nerve, that's all I can say, stranding me at that party, leaving me to fend for myself." His voice sank, and as Diana peered into his eyes she got the strangest feeling he was far more disarmed now than he'd been when she'd sprayed him with Mace.

"David, why are you here?" she asked squarely.

He looked aside, frustration tightening his features. Had Abbie been right when she'd said David would come around? Did Diana dare let herself think that the flowers he'd sent were not about death but about life and new beginnings?

Suddenly he gripped her arms, his fingers pressing into her soft flesh almost painfully. "Di, you have to come back with me."

Her eyes widened. "Why? Is something wrong at Cliff Haven?"

"Yes, everything—now that you're not there." Then he pulled her against him and kissed her with a fierceness that caused reverberations all the way down to her toes.

"Di, we have to talk," he whispered when he finally lifted his head.

Limp as a rag doll, she nodded and wondered where her anger had gone. "Let's go sit outside," she suggested, reaching for his hand.

They walked out to the porch swing and sat. Her hand, gripped within his, rested on his hard thigh.

"First of all," he began, "I have to apologize for everything I've ever said or done to hurt you. I put you through hell this summer." He laughed bitterly. "I still don't believe how I treated you when we first met. How pompous and—"

"David, please. That's history."

He nodded with strong conviction. "Yes. It is. But I still feel the need to apologize. For other things, too. The way I constantly shut you out whenever you tried to help, and then the other day at the stable, accusing you of inviting Walter, and those things I said..." He looked away, his eyes narrowed as if in pain.

In spite of his apparent contrition, she dredged up yet one more scowl. "Yes. You really outdid yourself that time, David. Though I suppose you had good reason to suspect me," she admitted, relenting a little. "I was the one who pushed the idea of the party on you. I was the one who sent out the invitations. It was a logical assumption."

His eyes raced over her face, seemingly trying to measure the depth of her sincerity. But even as she watched him, his expression changed.

"Lord, but you're beautiful!" he said.

Diana blushed right up to her hairline with the unexpectedness of the compliment.

Then his lips tightened into a grimace. "I no more want you out of my life than I want to stop living."

Diana lowered her head to his shoulder with a small shuddering sigh.

"It's just that a lot happened to me this summer," he explained, stroking her hair, "and I always seemed two steps behind, trying to adjust. But I did, always. Sometimes it took a few days, but I always came back. Didn't I?"

Diana raised her head and nodded thoughtfully.

"Having Walter and Glenda show up was obviously the biggest shock. Everything inside me short-circuited."

"That's what you get for letting unresolved problems fester too long. As maddening as my brothers can get, that's one thing I love about them. They've always made me talk about my problems, cry, scream, whatever it took."

"You're right. Walter and I should've had it out years ago."

"I'm always right. Haven't you figured that out by now?"

A tentative smile flickered across his handsome features. They sat quietly for a moment, listening to the thin creak of the swing as it rocked.

"David?" she finally said. "Why didn't you come to the carriage house yesterday and say all this?"

He frowned. "I figured you wouldn't talk to me." He turned to look at her, a glimmer of a smile in his eyes. "I did venture over in the afternoon, though, but you weren't around. So I decided to wait for the party. The plan was, I was going to dazzle you into forgiving me, sweep you off your feet with my charm and sparkling conversation..."

He paused and his expression darkened again. "Why did you do it, Di? Why did you leave?"

Diana suddenly realized how uncharacteristic this conversation was. David was doing almost all the talking, all the reaching out. Things had indeed turned around in the past few weeks.

"Did you decide you'd had enough of me? Did you give up?" he went on, his face grim, ready to hear the worst.

She lifted her chin stoically, pulling in a fortifying breath. "It...it was Glenda."

David sat silent for one brittle moment. Then, "What?" he said, his voice an octave higher than normal.

"It's okay. I understand," she said, squeezing his hand. "You don't have to pretend anymore. I know all about her. I saw the family albums. I read the newspaper clippings. I know how much you loved her and how you've suffered since she left you for Walter." An ache was tightening across her chest. "I also know she's been the driving force behind your success. You've amassed a fortune of your own to impress her and show her what she gave up. She's the reason you refuse to get involved with any other women."

David took her by the shoulders, turning her to face him. "But I am involved with another woman."

"Are you?" Her breath trembled.

His eyes narrowed, and his jaw set into a hard line. "Go on. What else do you know about me and Glenda? I'm dying to hear this."

She lowered her eyes. "Well, it's pretty obvious you're still carrying a torch for her. If you could have seen your face when she and Walter arrived, you'd know what I mean."

He let her go and sat forward, resting his elbows on his knees. "For heaven's sake, Di! Those two people betrayed me, humiliated me. They rearranged my entire life. And suddenly there they were after a thirteen-year cold war. You may have seen something in my face, but believe me, it was nothing more than an urge to maim."

"But . . . but I saw you walking with her the next day."

He laughed bitterly. "And could you also hear our conversation?"

"No, but you certainly looked happy and content." Her throat was tightening up on her, and speaking was becoming painful.

"Right again, Miss Know-It-All! But it was only because I'd finally aired all the ugly feelings I'd been harboring toward her and my brother—something I never would have done even a month ago, I should add. I felt free, released.''

''That's all?''

''Yes.''

Diana still wasn't completely convinced. ''So, have you reconciled?''

''I'm not really sure. They apologized to me and Evelyn, which came as no little shock, and Walter's invited me down to Maplecroft. Maybe we were just being polite for Cissy's sake. I don't know. Time will tell.'' He paused and slowly a smile entered his deep blue eyes. ''So, you think I've been languishing for my brother's wife all these years?''

''Yes, I do.'' Diana looked away, chewing her lip nervously.

''Okay, I'll admit she had an effect on me. I was hurt when we broke up, and I was madder than hell. I became bitter and started down a road of meaningless affairs. But it was a short road. It ended. Unfortunately a lot of people like to keep a reputation alive. But honestly, I'm not like that anymore. I haven't been for years. What I have been, I'll admit, is very guarded. And sure, Glenda is part of the reason, but just a small part. I simply reached the point where I didn't want *anyone* to get close.

''In any case, I don't ever want you thinking you're playing second fiddle to some ghost from my past. I got over Glenda years ago—quite thoroughly, too.''

''Well, how was I supposed to know? You never told me. You refused to talk about her.''

He blew out a sigh of frustration. ''I know. But I hope you'll understand. I stopped talking about my private life long ago. My late teens, early twenties—that was a terrible time for me, very emotional. I used to talk to reporters back then, but things always seemed to get misquoted or distorted. And even when they were right, I found it hurt to have my private life played out in public. I found it debasing, putting my feelings out there for everyone to discuss. I soon became defensive whenever anyone questioned me on a personal matter. Eventually I got downright nasty. What I didn't realize was that my defensiveness would cause such misunderstanding between you and me. I'll never shut you out again. I promise. Hey!'' He lifted her chin so that she had to look up at him. ''If you thought I was languishing for Glenda, what did you think was happening between you and me?''

''I wasn't sure. Sometimes I let myself believe it was real. Most times, though, I followed the general consensus—that you don't get involved romantically. You said it yourself, remember?''

''Sure do.''

''And it's okay if that's the case. I don't want you cushioning the blow because of guilt or a sense of obligation. I'm a big girl. I can handle it.'' She hoped he didn't notice her lips trembling.

David gazed at her a long quiet time. ''How about a lifetime commitment? Can you handle that, too?''

Diana opened her mouth and some sort of sound came out, but she was sure it was nothing decipherable.

''Di, I love you! I love you so much. Please, don't *ever* leave me again!'' His voice vibrated with tenderness and longing. Suddenly she was in his arms and they were clinging to each other as if they would never let go.

''I love you, too, David. I always will.'' She'd never had the chance to say those words aloud before, and as she did now, a tide of happiness engulfed her.

David sat back and reached into his jeans pocket. From it, he pulled out a blue velvet ring box. It swam out of focus as she gazed through her tears.

"I was planning to give you this last night—one of the reasons I apparently looked so happy yesterday." Irony seasoned his words.

Diana peered into his eyes, stupefied. The boyish eagerness she'd seen in his face, the easy charm, the peace—it had all been because of her?

He opened the box and took out a large emerald-cut diamond. "Will you marry me, Di? Will you *please* marry me and put me out of my misery?"

She laughed and sobbed, wondering if he believed she might actually consider saying no.

"Yes, I'll marry you."

He slipped the ring on her finger, then gathered her into his arms. "You've made me the happiest man alive," he said, laughing with relief. "I don't mean to rush you. I know you went through this whole wedding thing just last summer."

"I beg your pardon, but I'll rush if I want to." She wrapped her arms around his neck as tight as she could, drinking in the musky scent of his hair, the warmth of his rough cheek.

"Do you mean that?"

"I certainly do. I have one question, though. You *are* going to keep the house in Newport, aren't you?"

"Do you really have to ask?" He undid the belt around her waist and slipped his hand under her robe.

She tried to control her reaction, because there was still so much to talk about, but she knew he could feel her shudder. "David, would you mind if I kept teaching after we were married? Not here at Fairview..." She had to stop talking; his caresses were robbing her of her breath.

"Go on," he whispered, kissing her ear.

"N-not here. In Newp-port. I was thinking... Oh, David!" She dug her fingers into his hair, drawing him into a kiss.

When his lips finally released hers, there wasn't a coherent thought left in her head. And when he murmured, "Sure, anything you say," she had no idea what he was referring to.

"I think we ought to go inside, Di, unless you have very liberal-minded neighbors." He smiled as he nibbled the corner of her mouth.

"Yes, yes, of course." Diana clung to him as they rose from the swing. But as they were passing through the door, she grabbed the lintel and spun around.

"David, what are you doing with a helicopter?"

"Oh, do you like it? I was going to surprise you. It's for commuting. I plan to cut back on my business trips—send other people in my place. But I'll still have to show up at the office occasionally. I figure we can build a helipad at Cliff Haven easily enough. What do you think?"

"I..." She began to laugh. "I think I can't wait to get back."

"We can be there in an hour." He glanced into her eyes and began to smile wickedly. "Better make that two hours," he said, pulling her against him.

Just as his lips touched hers, however, a car turned into the driveway. Then another.

Diana groaned. "No, love. I'd say we're not going to get out of here for at least another three days. You're about to meet my brothers."

Fall in love with

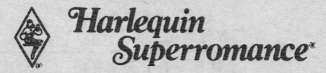

Harlequin Superromance®

Passionate.
Love that strikes like lightning. Drama that will touch your heart.

Provocative.
As new and exciting as today's headlines.

Poignant.
Stories of men and women like you. People who affirm the values of loving, caring and commitment in today's complex world.

At 300 pages, Superromance novels will give you even more hours of enjoyment.

Look for four new titles every month.

Harlequin Superromance
"Books that will make you laugh and cry."

HARLEQUIN

Romance®

**This October,
travel to England with
Harlequin Romance
FIRST CLASS title #3155
TRAPPED
by Margaret Mayo**

"I'm my own boss now and I intend to stay that way."

Candra Drake loved her life of freedom on her narrow-boat home and was determined to pursue her career as a company secretary free from the influence of any domineering man. Then enigmatic, arrogant Simeon Sterne breezed into her life, forcing her to move and threatening a complete takeover of her territory and her heart....

Harlequin Intrigue®

Trust No One...

When you are outwitting a cunning killer, confronting dark secrets or unmasking a devious imposter, it's hard to know whom to trust. Strong arms reach out to embrace you—but are they a safe harbor...or a tiger's den?

When you're on the run, do you dare to fall in love?

For heart-stopping suspense and heart-stirring romance, read Harlequin Intrigue. Two new titles each month.

HARLEQUIN INTRIGUE—where you can expect the unexpected.